Erotic Synergy

Goddess Circle Press, LLC
Goddesscirclepress.com

Copy editing by Gratitude of Winds

Cover design and graphic design by Anagram

ISBN-10:0988650614
ISBN-13:978-0-9886506-1-9

Contents

Art by Apollonia Saintclair

"I do not want to be the leader. I refuse to be the leader. I want to live darkly and richly in my femaleness. I want a man lying over me, always over me. His will, his pleasure, his desire, his life, his work, his sexuality the touchstone, the command, my pivot. I don't mind working, holding my ground intellectually, artistically; but as a woman, oh, God, as a woman I want to be dominated. I don't mind being told to stand on my own feet, not to cling, be all that I am capable of doing, but I am going to be pursued, fucked, possessed by the will of a male at his time, his bidding."

— *Anaïs Nin*

Introduction

Erotic Synergy was born out of the many conversations between two close friends who pondered, analyzed, revolted, desired, questioned and danced around the many ways we are erotic with ourselves and with others. As two grown females comfortable with our own sexual experience and aptitude we both were also troubled by the double standard that still very much exists about women who own and exercise their sexual freedom. We've encountered in our personal experiences people who enjoyed our sexual connection but then would use that against us during an argument and try to slut-shame us into our place, or just as bad, judge us silently for our sexual competence.

We strongly believe that women should be free to express their sexuality as they see fit, without apology, and have partners who support them in exploring all sides of themselves. In this collection, many of our writers decided to explore their sexuality through the lens of BDSM. In recent years the closeted world of BDSM (the common acronym for Bondage & Discipline / Domination & Submission / Sadism & Masochism) has come to mainstream media. Kink communities across the globe organize gatherings (aka munches), workshops, play parties, performances and even large conventions. There are many variations of what a BDSM relationship may look like. Perhaps the most important principle, regardless of roles and dynamics, is that BDSM play should always be consensual. At a kink workshop at Bound in Boston that we attended, the instructors covered the absolute importance and necessity of consent and knowledge of safety protocols at the beginning of the workshops. They would discuss ground rules that people should consider and implement before any scene begins, such as safe words, checking that the bottom (submissive partner) is not dehydrated, inquiring about any past injuries, off-limit areas of the body that shouldn't be touched or unclothed. BDSM should not be confused with abuse, as the participants are all consenting to engage in BDSM play.

In Erotic Synergy we look primarily to highlight women's, and also non-binary gendered people's, perspectives of erotic engagement. We selected short stories and poems that evoke a range of different scenarios and roles that people desire, dominate, experiment with and/or to which they actively submit. Most stories depart from heternormative behaviors and beliefs to explore non-conforming ways a person can be in an erotic context. Erotic Synergy is a literary and visual playground of many secret fantasies, which only few of us have actually dared to experience.

We thank our copy editor, Gratitude of Winds, and graphic design company Anagram for their skillful work and professionalism.

We thank our contributors for sharing their beautiful, powerful and engaging words, imagery, and art with us in this collection.

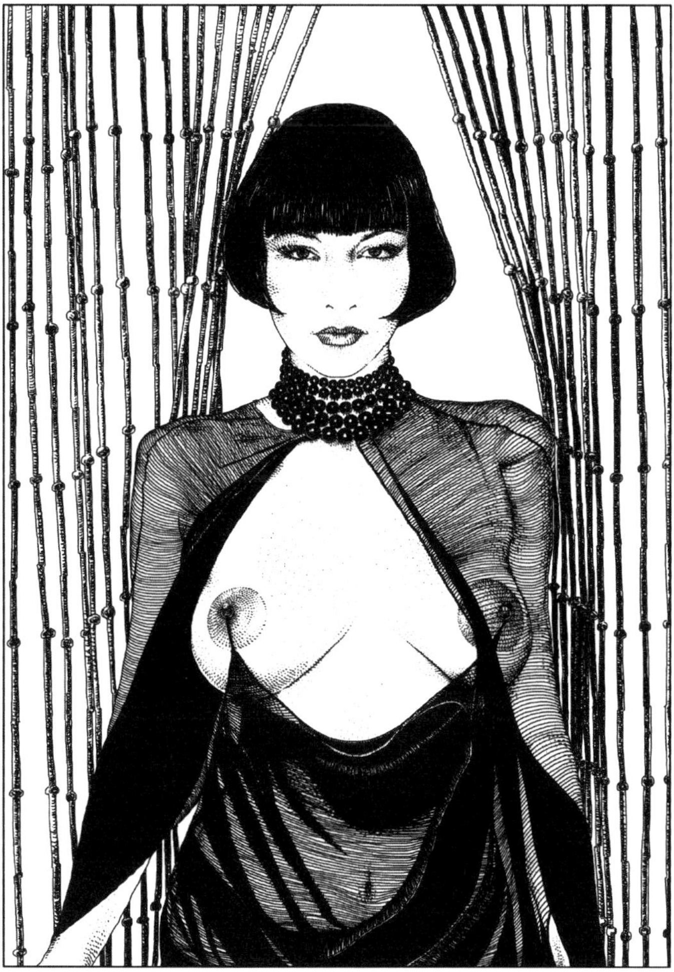

TAKE ME HOME

By Sorsha Rose

She whispered in his ear
"Take Me Home"
She didn't mean a physical place
It wasn't a palpable destination
It was a concept
A locational latitude in their minds
It was her hand in his
Or where they went together
When he whipped her into
Something resembling meringue
It was their eyes locked
Connected
Perceptive
Peering
Into the core of them
Every nuance peeled
Revealed
It was her cheek
Gently caressing his cock
Creating an embrace with her shoulder
It was the little bites he left
Scattered across her inner thighs
The exchange of energy
When he spanked her
And the mere moments that ticked by
Before she was soaring in space
Because there was a trust so profound
It was the visions they shared
Of potentiality
It was the regard granted
The intense attention
In bestowing their intentions

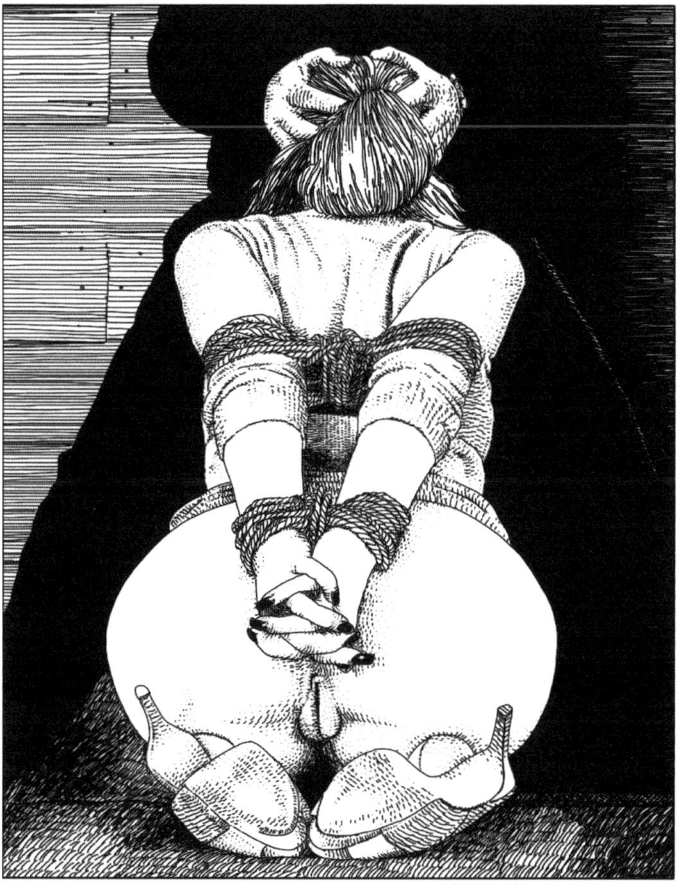

The symbols and gestures
They birthed meaning to
It was their sense of belonging
Feeling right
Encouraged
Accepted
And of being owned
Home

To be a Liberated Woman

By Diane Wright

To be a liberated woman (sexually, financially, emotionally, physically) does not come easy. Some would want to bask in her warm sensual light. Roll around in it, get the juiciness of it all over them. But if that opportunity is not made available to them specifically, and they know it is to another or worse to others, then watch out because then all the rough and tough arms of slut-shaming can start swinging. Yes, it's totally okay for you to be a slut (aka a sexually liberated woman) with them, but the moment you are not, then you are just a piece of shit immoral whore.

What's a woman to do? Here she is with an awaken libido that's been suppressed for way too long. Suddenly the multiple orgasms and intense far-shooting ejaculations are literally within her grasp.

Surveillance comes into play. A city gal displaced in a small town. Watchful eyes, all about her. Judging and scrutinizing her non-Christian ways. What does she want? FREEDOM (yes, it does need to be all in caps). Freedom to be a self-actualized adult. At mid-life does permission need to be had, when you're female and of color? In this beloved US of A, yes most certainly according to many. Chains do not slip off so easily. Invisible constraints do indeed exist.

So where, how, does one move into peace? Dream of floating in and above clouds, that not only support her, but wish her to soar.
Where, how, when?
Questions.
One sits. Learns how to sit, especially when skittish from trauma.
Wait for stillness to kiss the mind and wish her peace.

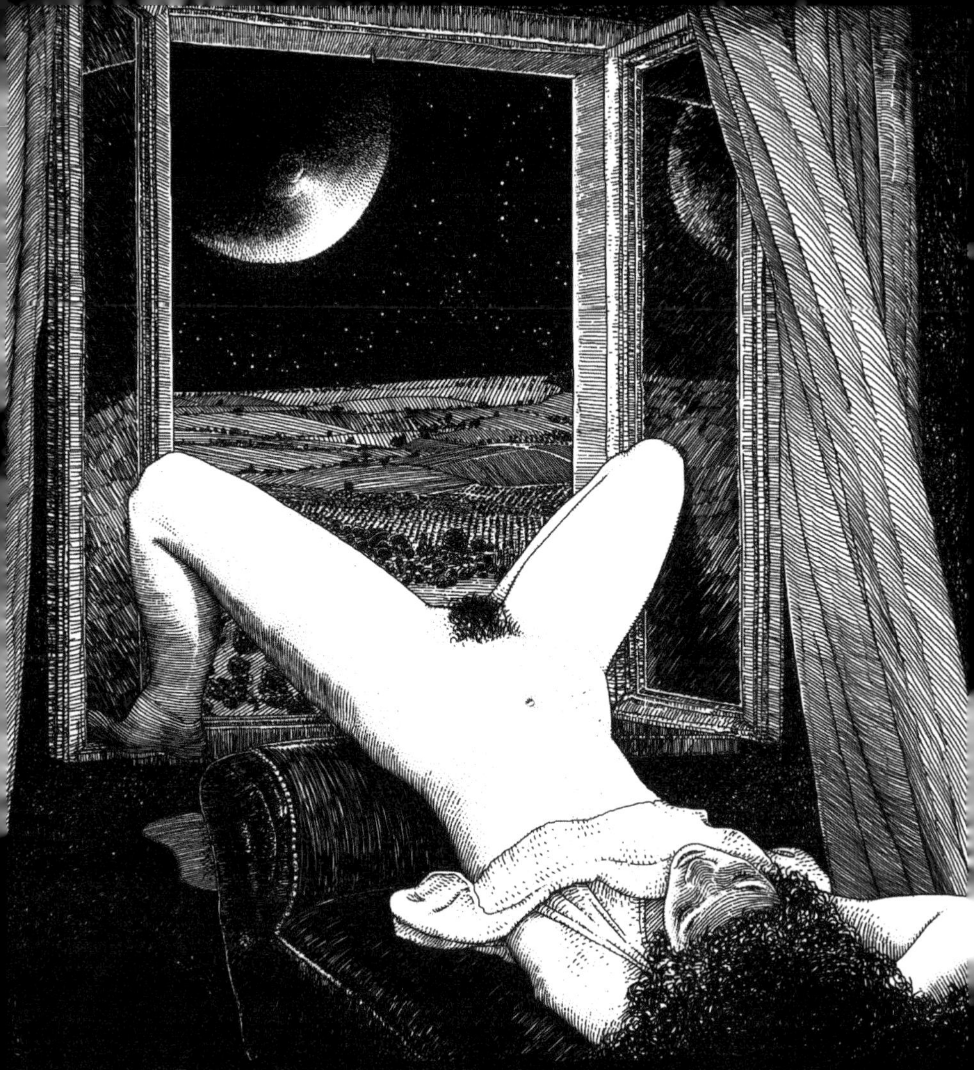

Procrastination

By Northern Star

Trying to work. Futile.
In truth I think I would prefer
To impale myself upon your hardened cock
Feel you fill me, stretching my
Capacity to need
Juices flowing
As I hold you
Deep inside
No wild thrusting, not yet
Just this
Firm pulsing
Of my muscles
Engulfing you
Drawing you
Deeper
Touching that place
That aches
For release
“There, yes” whispered
As I cling tightly to you
“Ohhh... yes, more please”
As urgency increases
“Please” breathless, barely heard
Until at last, I give way
Let you take over
Rolling on top of me
The better
To drive
Deep
Hard
Passions flowing
Fuck yes, no lady now

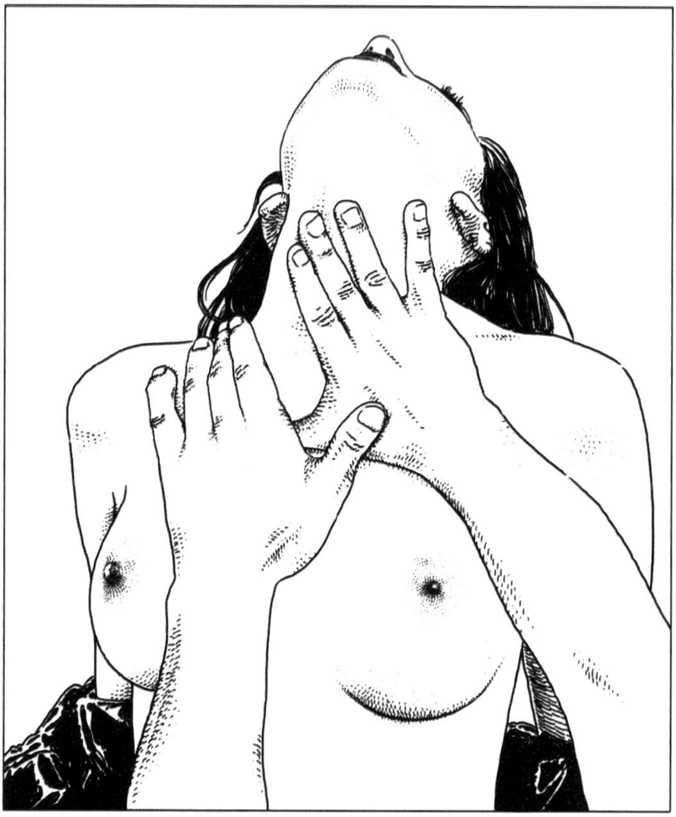

Harder, biting into your shoulder
To suppress the scream that wills
To shake
The very
Window panes
"FUCK ME!!!'"

And such.

Good Boy

By SisterT

I bounce slightly to the pulsing drumbeat. The music has me in a playful mood and I delight in the fact that it covers the sounds of my movements. A click here, a tighter tie there. Once you are arranged just so, I lower the volume, step back and admire the view. Blindfolded and naked. Facing the wall, arms above your head. I've told you nothing of my plans. All you have to do is what I say.

"Spread your legs." I run my fingers up the inside of your thighs and tickle your balls. I can hear you moan a little and I smile. Sliding my hand into your hair and holding you firmly, I slowly press my breasts against your back. When I thrust myself forward and push you against the wall, you are definitely caught unaware. I pull away and deliver a sound smack to your right cheek, leaving my hand on your skin, pressing in the sensation. You catch your breath. I repeat on the other cheek. This time you grunt but otherwise stay silent. I come up close and whisper in your ear how pleased I am with you. Such a good boy.

I reach around and take your already hard cock in my hand. A couple of deliberate strokes and then I rub my finger across the tip. As expected, you're leaking. I milk a little onto my fingertips and tell you to open up. Slipping my wet fingers into your mouth, I tell you to lick them clean, slowly. I make a few more trips to your cock and then back to your mouth. Such a talented tongue. The next time my fingers enter your mouth I see you pause only momentarily as you notice that the taste is different.

"Watching you has made me very, very wet..." The mirth in my voice is unmistakable.

I lower your hands and have you bend over at the waist, presenting your ass nicely. You can hear me talking but I know you aren't paying attention. You are trying to concentrate on the sounds you are hearing. Is that a belt? Are those buckles being fastened? Could that be more restraints? What is that? I end the suspense. "I want

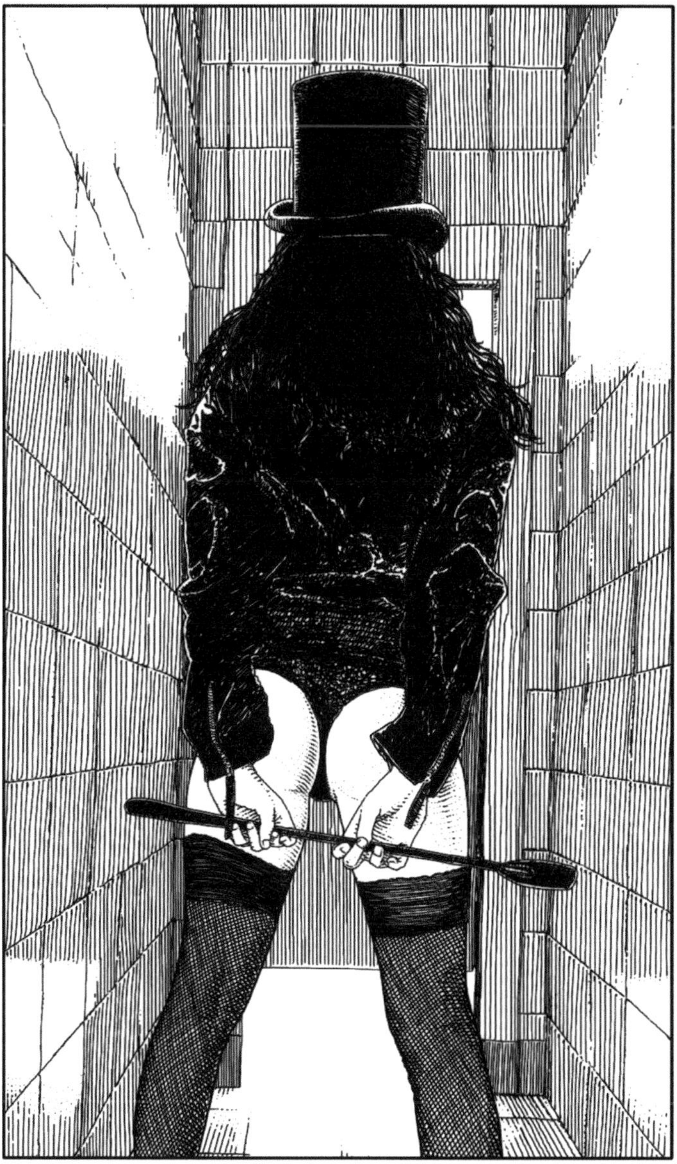

that mouth again. Open up and get my cock good and wet." Your mouth falls open immediately. You are eager to please. At first I let you work on the tip of the strap-on before gently sliding myself in and out of your lips. You are a talented little cock sucker. Your lips and tongue lavish the dildo with such desire and affection, I get even more aroused. You are terribly sexy but I have to shake myself from my reverie. The night is young and I have lots more planned for you. Stepping away I swear you look disappointed.

I walk behind you. "Such a good boy deserves special attention, don't you agree?" You say nothing but I can see you trembling. I let spit drip from my mouth and fall onto your asshole, rubbing it around and inside a bit before letting the head of my cock slip inside. You almost stand on your toes as I move in and out, each stroke just a little deeper. Once I've taken you fully, I begin fucking you in earnest. You try to hold back from making a sound but a swift swat on your ass, and me telling you that I will leave you like this unless I start hearing some noise, gets you moaning with abandon. Such a good boy.

I pull out of you and squat down to see your cock. You are painfully hard, pre-cum almost pouring from you. The minute I touch you, you shudder, which pleases me immensely. I wrap my fingers around you and begin to stroke. "No cumming without my permission. You have to ask me first. Don't you dare cum on your own." You say nothing but nod your head in understanding, your face screwed up in determination. My stroking gets you panting harder and harder. I can tell you're trying to hold on but it's not easy. Every time I think you're close I change up. Slower, faster, just stroke the tip, stroke the whole shaft. Your whole body is shaking and you finally reach the point of no return, begging me for release. "Do you really need to cum?" I think you can barely concentrate at this point but you tell me yes. "I want to see you make yourself cum. Don't cum until I release your hands." Once your hands are freed, I watch you with interest as you jerk yourself off. Your orgasm comes hard and you scream out loud, collapsing to your knees, covered in sweat.

"Very nicely done. I enjoyed watching you. Now pull yourself together." I take one of your hands and place it on my wet pussy lips. "You've got a mess to clean up."

There is no mistaking the wicked pleasure in my voice.

My difference

By isobella

The Cloak and Dagger
on Wind Street
was bouncing
roofed, the
jazz singer in the centre
no Neil Diamond, however
drew much attention
the queue by the bar
of him/s and her/s
the ordinary folk
gossiping about work
shopping, the weather
mundane boring
conversations
were oblivious
they didn't see us
sitting in the corner
they failed to observe
his right hand up
my skirt
they didn't see him
finger me after he
dipped his digit
in his gin and tonic
they didn't know
when he whispered in
my ear..
'go to the loo and
insert your butt plug'
they couldn't tell
about the swell
of my cunt

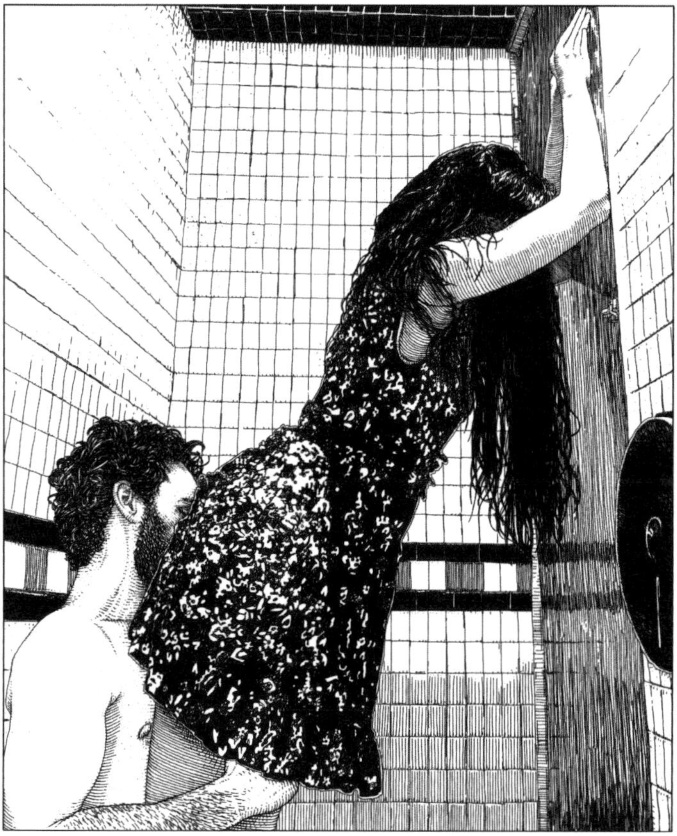

or the filthy mind thoughts
just as well
I strolled past them
bigger than my boots
just like a peacock
showing its feathers
and I bathed in the
knowledge and delight
of my difference

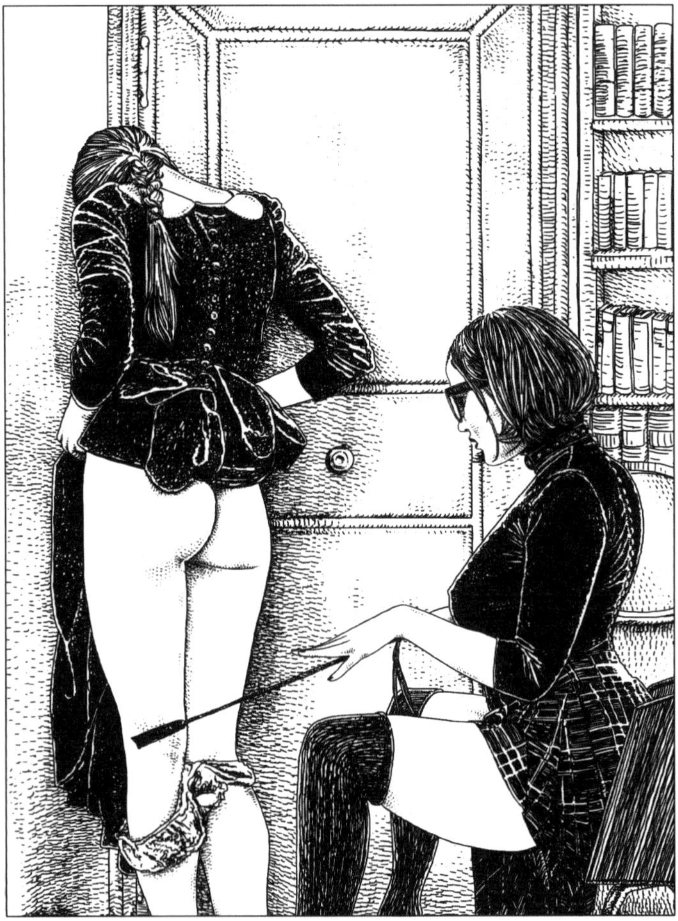

A Wicked Surprise

By Eleanor Regan

I should have known she was up to something when she asked to borrow a spare key for when she next visited. While it was a request I was happy to grant her, looking back I realize she was plotting and scheming, especially when she refused to identify exactly when she would be using the key. Visits came and went, and the key was never used. Weeks later I had completely forgotten she had it. When she announced one day she was popping over but didn't know when, which in itself was very odd behaviour, I still didn't put the puzzle together. Which meant she had me exactly where she wanted me. Not knowing when she would arrive or what she was coming over for, I just busied myself with housework and coffee breaks. Always a daydreamer, I was lost in thought as I stood waiting for the kettle to boil. I didn't hear the door go, or footsteps behind me, so I should have been terrified when a hand formed a fist in my hair, while another fast made its way under my skirt. Although my heart was pounding as my brain tried to figure out what was happening, I couldn't shut out the fact I had become instantly aroused.

It didn't take long for me to realize who it was. Her touch was distinctive, I could hear the familiar sound of her breath against my ear, but she was making sure I couldn't move to see her, my head controlled by her hand in my hair, my body wedged between her and the kitchen cupboards, as she used her fingers to bring me as close to climax as she could before stopping abruptly. Only then when she had removed her fingers from my pussy did she speak, and it was short and direct and gave little away.

'Don't move,'

Despite my curiosity being at an all time high, I knew better than to disobey her. I stood completely still, with my eyes closed for fear of catching an accidental glimpse of what she was up to. I didn't have to wait long for her to start organizing things though. As I stood there with my hands on my kitchen counter, she blindfolded me and removed all of my clothes. For a moment nothing happened, but I could feel how close she was to me, I could feel the desire moving between us like sparks of electricity and most noticeably of all I could feel my pussy dripping. I had no idea what she had planned, but I was very excited to find out.

The next contact between us was her hands reaching for my wrists and turning me to face into the room. Her hands then began to bind my own with rope. She didn't just bind my wrists though, she used that rope to bind my arms to my body, I could feel the fabric of the rope against my back, around my breasts, across my stomach, around my arms and any effort to move was pointless, my top half was completely restricted. She was in complete control, which was made even more clear when I felt a small tug pull me forward. As my feet slowly and cautiously took a step, she tugged again, and so we moved, tug by tug, step by step, slowly and carefully, until it became clear she was done with careful.

With one forceful tug I stumbled forward and felt myself caught in her grasp, she spun me round and moved me backwards and I could feel the bed cover against the back of my legs. Then she asked me a question that had no meaning, because I had no idea what was happening, but it was a question that without doubt only had one answer.

'Are you ready?'

'Yes,'

With that one small word she pushed me backwards onto the bed, and her hand began to tie again. I had no idea how she had tied me, or quite what position I was in. All I knew was that I was completely immobilised and my pussy was very much on show, and I knew that when she looked at me she would see I was glistening with desire. I was throbbing and tingling, and I hadn't even considered when she might touch me. Just knowing I was completely at her mercy and on display for her was working wonders for my arousal levels.

For the longest time she didn't touch me. She did play with me though. She played and teased and she pushed me so far into wanting her that I could feel it inside me like a desperate obsession. Still blindfolded so I couldn't see her, I heard her purposefully undressing, her clothes landing as she threw them down forcefully. All the while I was picturing her standing before me, her naked form slowly being revealed, item by item. I didn't mind being bound but I so wished I could see her. When I felt her climb onto the bed I thought at least there might be some kind of contact, to ease the torture of not being able to enjoy the view. I was out of luck, I was uncertain of her position, but I knew her body was just a hair's width away. I could feel her proximity, but I was bound so securely I couldn't move in anyway to make our bodies touch. The only sensation I felt was her whisper on my ear. So soft, so quiet and utterly arousing. For the longest time she whispered into my ear, deliberately explicit and picking up all the things I liked best, I was in awe of just how well planned this was.

'You look so fucking sexy, unable to move and just waiting to be played with. Do you know how wet you are? Your pussy is shining it's so wet. Dripping wet in fact. It's begging to be played with, begging to come, begging to be made wetter. But you've been so good, you haven't said a word. I'm very pleased. So pleased in fact, I am also very wet. That taste you love is dripping down my thighs, imagine how good it would feel to lick at my pussy, or to slide your fingers in. Remember those noises you love, I'd definitely make them right now. I wonder what noises you would make if I did those things to you right now.'

With that I felt her hand ever so softly against my pussy, her fingers slowly circling my clit, then slowly in and out of my pussy, it was excruciatingly and deliciously agonizing. I was desperate to grind against her and thrust my fingers deep into her pussy at the same time, yet there I was completely unable to do either. All I could do was moan, and gasp and wait as she continued to enjoy her toy. When she stopped I didn't know if I was grateful for the break or disappointed that the sweet torture had ceased.

'I need you to do something for me, then I promise I will fuck you properly, do you think you can do it? You will find it hard, and it will make you desperate to be untied, but I won't do it. Do you think you can do this one thing for me?'

'Yes, anything, I'll do anything.'

'That is what I like to hear.'

I always cursed myself for that, I was big on promising 'anything', thankfully I'd never had this tested with a task that was unpleasant and today's task was about as pleasant as it could get, but she was right, it made me beyond desperate to be untied. I wanted to be untied so I could fuck her properly, so I could spread her legs, and grab her boobs, I wanted to be free to grab her arse and pull her to me, I wanted to grab her hair and pull her into a passionate kiss, I wanted to pin her down and fuck her until she begged me to stop, but all I could do was as she asked, and I did it like a wild woman who had been starved for the longest time.

'Fuck me with your tongue.'

As she made her request she straddled my face and lowered her pussy to my mouth, my tongue eagerly reaching out to taste her. Fuck! She was wet. So wet. I could feel her juices on my lips, my chin, my nose. She wasn't lying when she said was turned on, and having me bound beneath her licking at her pussy, seemed to be turning her on a whole lot more. I licked, I sucked, I nibbled and she ground her pussy into my face with a force I had never experienced. I could feel her own face was inches from my own throbbing, aching wetness. I could not wait to have her mouth on me and her fingers inside me.
In what could only be described as a flurry of orgasms and fucking, she started to climax and fuck me simultaneously. As she moaned and pushed down onto my mouth, her fingers pushed deep into me. Gone were the slow, deliberate movements. This was fast, deep and relentless. My body felt like it would burst from her expertly tied restraints, as the pressure inside me grew. Instead her tongue and fingers pushed me into an orgasm that made me feel like every organ was buzzing and shuddering, my skin was tingling from head to toe and I felt the pressure in my pussy release as I squirted, her fingers still pushing in and out causing it to spray in all directions. I was well and truly fucked. She had certainly kept her promise.

Gradually she started to untie me, and once I was completely free from restraints but my blindfold remained I was asked to stay still just for a moment. Nothing happened though and moments later my blindfold was removed. I wanted to ask why she'd ask me to stay still some more, but in my orgasmic haze I could barely remember my name, let alone remember to ask questions. So instead I just lay there as she traced the marks the rope had left on my flesh.

'You looked so lovely all tied up in that rope, and I love the marks it's left behind. Thank you for trusting me today.'

'I trust you always and I should be thanking you really, for an amazing time. I do wish I could have seen how I was tied though and how it looked. It sounds pretty.'
'I'll try and remember you'd like to see next time.'

With that she softly kissed me and moments later I was fast asleep.

A week or so later, on another visit, she handed me my key back. Along with a beautifully wrapped parcel.

'You can keep the key if you want, it's silly to have you knocking really.'

'It is, a little. This way though, whenever I ask for it, you'll know I have something planned. But—and this is a big but—it won't ever be the same thing twice and until it happens you'll always be wondering.'

She had a point. It was a delightfully wicked game to play.

'And if you open your parcel, you will realize you have something to help keep the memory of the last time quite vivid in your mind.'

As I slowly unwrapped my gift I found a beautiful book, bound in a very thin silky rope. When I opened it my mind struggled to understand what it was seeing. I immediately recognized the person as me, but the images were unlike any I had ever seen before. Suddenly my brain engaged and I understood, she had taken pictures of everything. From me stood naked in my kitchen, right up to the point she had asked me to lie still and I hadn't known why. It was one of the most wonderful gifts I'd ever been given and every time I looked at it I hoped she'd ask for my key again. The months came and went though, and no request was made, I had begun to think it was a one time thing. It never occurred to me to check the key was still where I kept it. Had I done so I might have been a little more prepared for the next adventure she had planned.

The Coat

By Tori Chatfield

Drifting through the world
With carefree steps
She tangled and teased
Loved and lost
And loved again.
Walking forward -
Never ever looking back
She gathered experience,
Wrapped it around her
And wore it as a coat.
Its fabric was rich and full
Soft velvet, warm fur,
Sparkling organza -
Encrusted with gems
And lined with silk.
Every thread, every strand
Was woven in perfectly.
Each encounter
Picked out in golden beads
And displayed proudly.
Yet as she walked on
She left pieces of herself behind.
Slowly she became the coat
And it became her
Until the coat was all that remained.

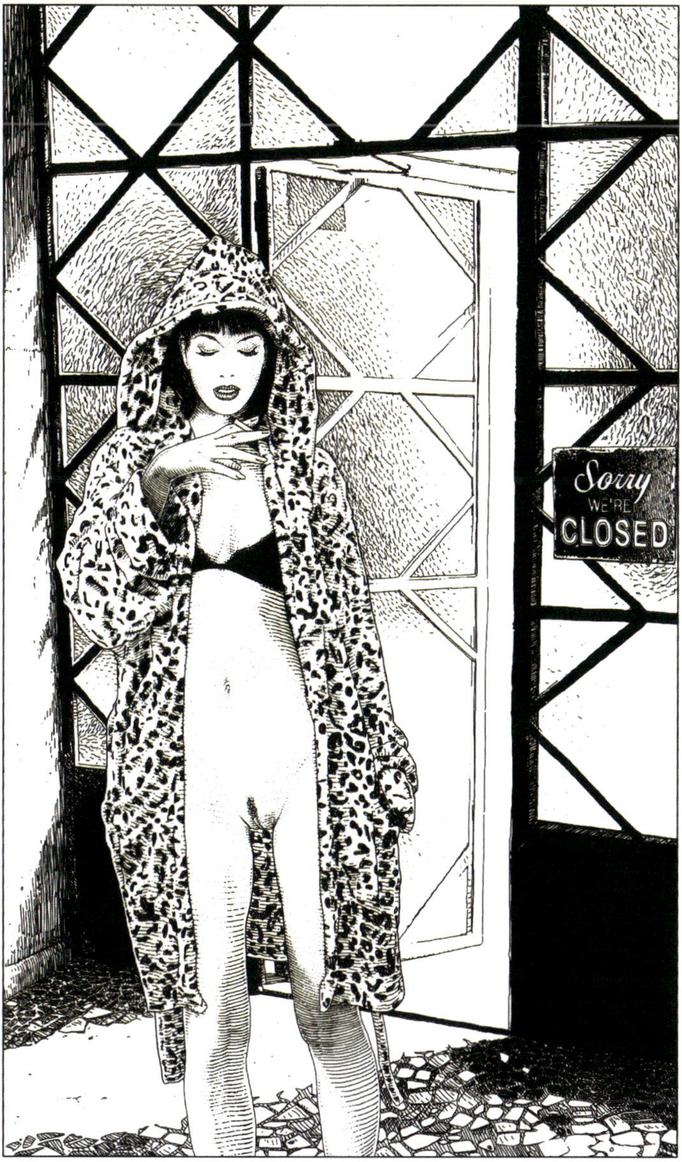
Sorry
WE'RE
CLOSED

I'd appreciate it

By Leaena

I would appreciate it if you'd
run your filthy hands
all over my soul
leave it in tatters
wrecked beyond repair

I would appreciate it if you'd
whisper obscene verse
into my ears making
me blush like a ripe
and juicy berry

I would appreciate it if you'd
breathe bruises onto my skin
a ravaging kiss of leather
forcing screams of pleasure
to pass lips bitten and bloody

I'd really appreciate it

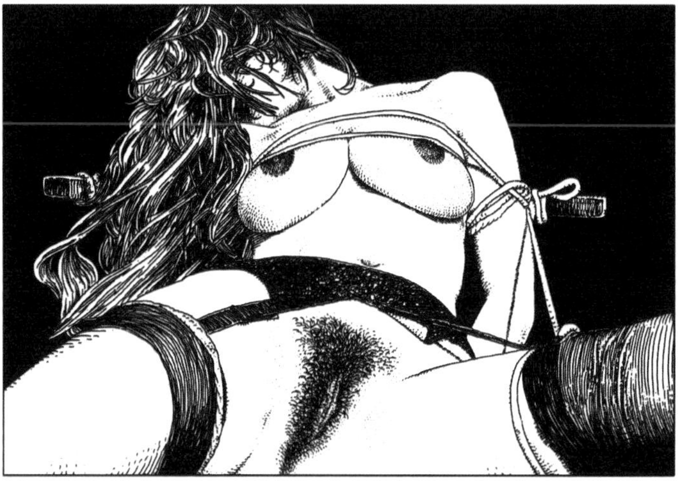

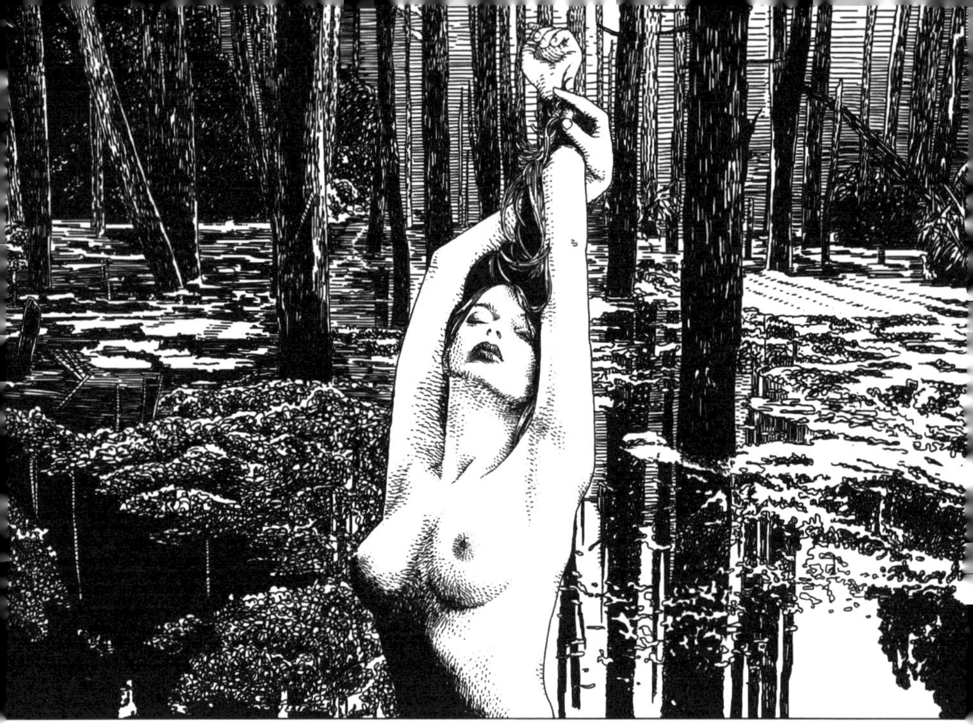

Ties that Bind

By Northern Star

Seeing into his darkest thoughts,
she sees,
this wish he has
to be devoured.
Wondering, how tightly
must the ropes be tied,
to keep him pinned,
still,
while she slowly
and most intently
explores all.
His neck, the salty taste
of lust warmed skin,
the hollow of his throat,
nipples, sensitive to strokes of tongue

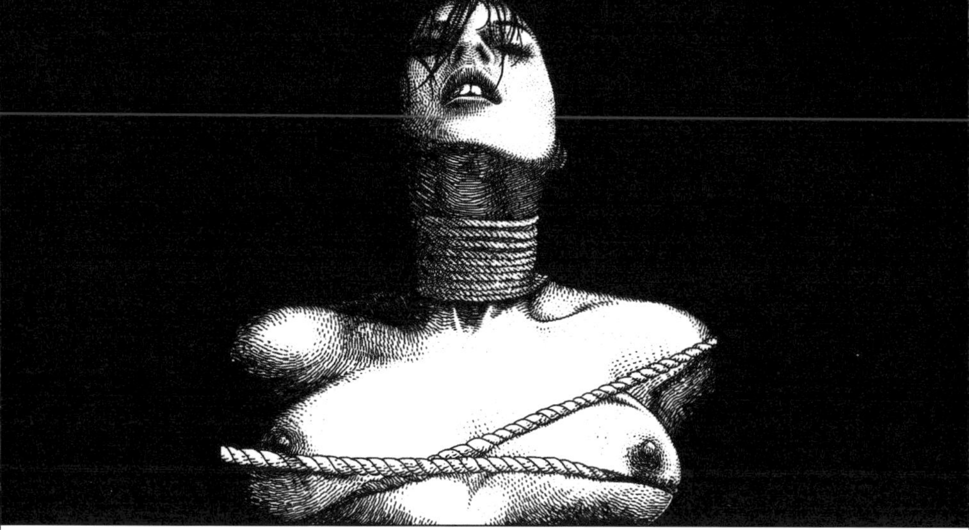

And abdomen, much used
To work
But not to softened lips.
How hard will he
Strain against
The ties that bind
As she grows ever nearer
Her breath hot
Her hungry mouth
Sensuous
How hard will he strain
As her tongue
So delicately
Begins
To map the curves
And lines
Of this instrument
Of her pleasure

Musings of a Feminist Submissive

By Sasha Lewis

There is an inner conflict in many women, including myself...the desire to be strong and powerful women, making our own way in the world wrestling with the desire to be submissive to our lovers in the bedroom. For a while, it was a conflict I greatly struggled with... how can I be a strong feminist, if I still feel this intense need to be subservient to a man sexually? The traits that I find almost abhorrent in men during daylight hours—hyper-masculinity, selfishness, authoritarianism—are the same that make my pussy drip in the bedroom. So the question becomes twofold. Is it possible for me to reconcile both sides of myself and have them live side by side? And is it possible to find a man who can tap into that hyper-masculinity in the bedroom, but will shut it off or tamp it down when he is being my partner in our life, outside of the bedroom? So far, I have not been successful in finding this elusive man... But I have come to terms with myself. For me, being a feminist means that women can choose what they want in all aspects of their life. Accepting my submissive side has made me feel stronger in my sexual power, not weaker. The bigger problem is finding a man who is worth submitting to...

Kitten Gets the Bell

By Olivia Hellbond

Kitten sat patiently on the sofa wearing Master's favorite satin sheer thigh high stockings with velvet emerald bows on the front of them. Black velvet 6in baby doll heels. They always gave her legs a magical touch to them, making the shape of them stand out more and giving her that "legs for days" look. The stockings were held up by matching emerald garters which were attached to the crotchless panties he loved seeing her in.

He told her to be ready for him in a "present" matter, making special note of the quotations marks. So she bought velvet emerald fabric and fashioned it into a giant bow which was wrapped around her breast. She made it tight giving her girls a peek-a-boo effect for him to admire. She always wore cat ears that matched everything she wore and let her hair hang in lazy black waves down her back and shoulders. She knew her hazel eyes had changed colors to match the emerald she was wearing. Something that she knew he would adore.

A tiny little jiggle from a bell brought a smile to her face as she watched her Master walk out of his office. He had a look of stress, which was quickly replaced by desire for his favorite little kitten.

"Come to me kitten." His words were full of adoration. She hugged herself inside every time he called her "kitten." Slowly she got on all fours and was going to approach him as he always wanted her to. But he put his hand up and gestured for her to rise and walk toward him.

Daring not to disobey she gracefully stood up and walked toward him in the quickest of steps. His hand immediately went for the small of her back, bringing her in for a deep kiss. She moaned into his lips enjoying the familiar sweet taste of his English Breakfast Tea with a hint of mint.

"You look of a fine royal jewel in all of this emerald. It pleases me that you envisioned what I was looking for." He said this while taking a step back to admire her more closely, but suddenly frowned.

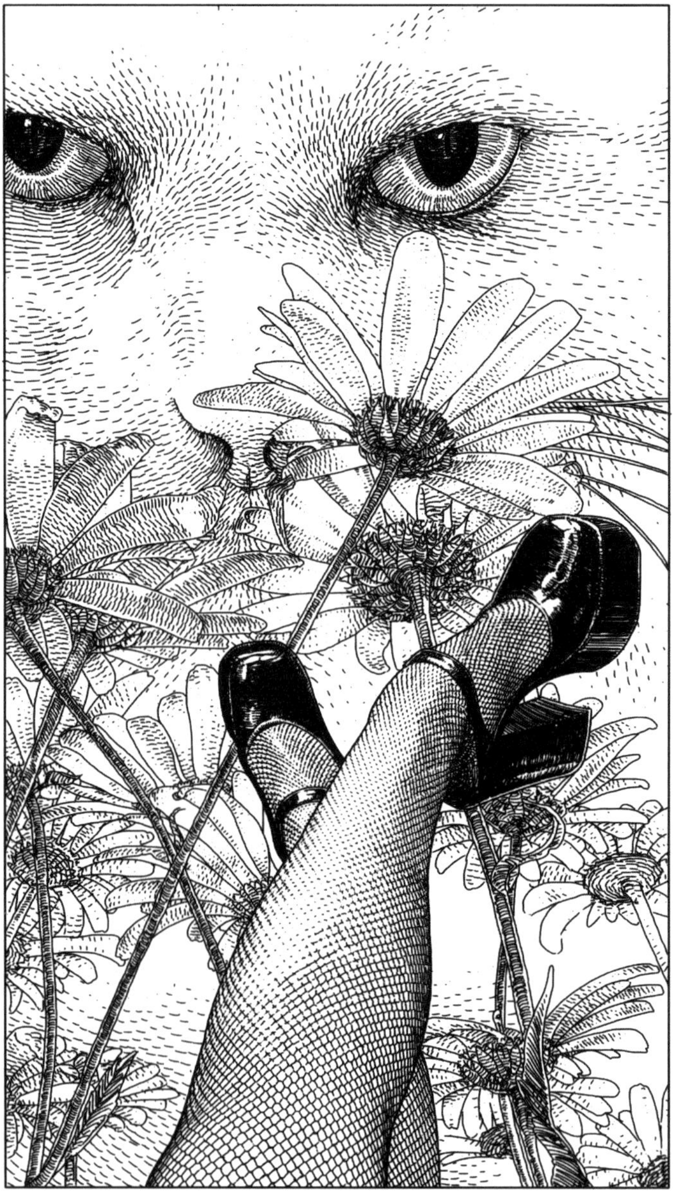

"Yet something is still missing from you that I am not quite happy with."

A pit of sadness washed over the brilliant glow she was radiating. What had she forgotten? Surely she had done everything she was told? With a look of confusion and disappointment she asked him, "Master?..." She saw his hand reach behind his back, and felt a slight tightness of her stomach, thinking she was going to be spanked.

She heard the familiar jiggle yet again. He pulled from behind him a velvet black box and opened it. Inside was black satin ribbon with gold chains on each end, and in the middle a big gold bell.

"My sweet little kitten has been needing this for a while. Figured I make sure it was the perfect one for you and only you."

Oh he truly did love her and she knew it. She couldn't help the scream of joy that escaped her lips, nor did Master mind. In fact he was hoping for this very reaction as he placed her brand new bell around her neck.

His arms around her petite waist, she felt the warmth of his breath brush over her naked shoulders. And he whispered into her ear, "Now my perfect little kitten let's open up my gift."

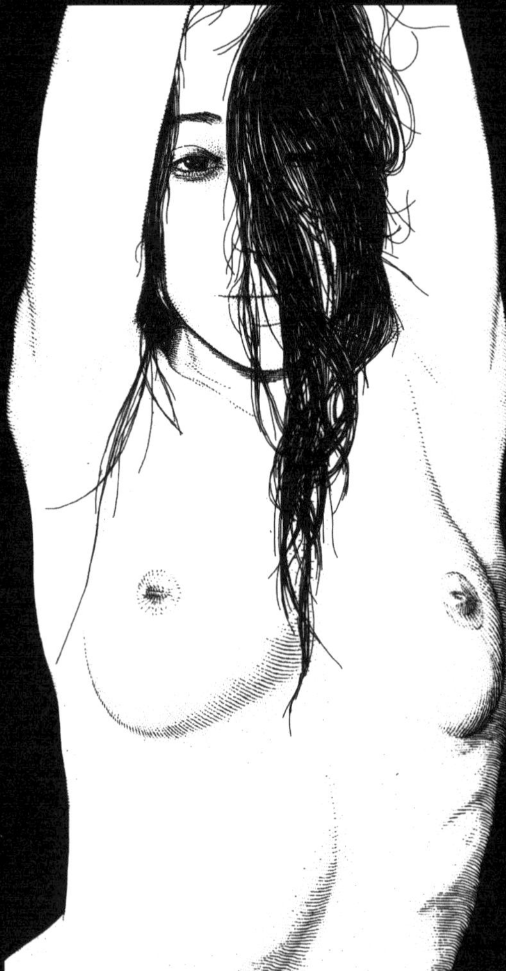

the submissive

By Nocturne Noir

her submissiveness
beautifully
painfully
unique
a deep natural compulsion
to fulfill your desires
a dual mutual desiderata.
take away your puny overbearing esteem
she's not for the weak
not to be pistol whipped
used, abused
and abandoned.
enormous efforts from your part:
strength, wisdom, patience, experience
to penetrate her walls
loosen the chokehold
of her self-protective mechanisms
accept her flaws
soak up her affections.
Know her core
Bring her to inner peace
Damage not her trust
she is canny in her psychic sense
unbridled by your fabricated lies.
Chisel away the complex
to possess her
preserving persistence
absolute trust
don't deceive
strip her away
break her hallowing silence
rip quietly, deliberately, progressively

down her inhibitions
teach her what she wants
expand her
goals and knowledge.
comprehend all you do
affect her properly
sanction the safety level
limits and consistency
the sacred, profound responsibility
express the capability
to correct, forgive, reassure and love
to master, to accept her universal force
respect her precious gift.
It's not about desire
sex or control.
It's about absolute devotion
for the submissive.

Aspiring Cock Worshiping Artist

By Sorsha Rose

They were lounging in bed
After hours of body love
That lit them up from the outside in
She was splayed on top of him
Her chin resting on her arms
With her hands lying lazily
Across his upper abdomen

She said, "I have loved three cocks in my life
I mean love to look, feel, smell,
Must have near me
Can't get enough of this gorgeous cock, love"

He smiled as she continued talking
"Has anyone loved your cock as much as I have?"

"No," He replied.

"How do you know?" she queried.

He said, "Because they didn't show it"

Her eyes went wide as she spoke
"I want to line them all up
Show them what it is to worship your cock
Allow them to make up for their shameful neglect
And then tell them to, "Get out!"

He laughed, but she was serious
She could not begin to comprehend

Being in the presence
Of such a beautiful man you loved
With such a gorgeous cock
And not kissing it all over
From tip, to balls, to perineum
Not running their tongue along
That sweet spot of veins behind the head
Not letting the tip go in and out just at the top
Moving their tongue along that ridge
Taking it in to the hilt
And then swallowing a little more
Rubbing it lovingly against their cheek
Making it the wettest endeavor
Allowing him to fuck their face with abandon
Swallowing him so deep, and then deeper still
Getting long strings of drool to refract in light
Making him feel like there is no place
They would rather be
That this was a spiritual act of true worship

Every chance she had to show him this she did
An honest gasp at first sight
The deep inhale of his delicious musk man scent
That made her mouth water
There had even been moments
When just seeing his cock brought her to tears
She was as emotionally attached to his cock
As she was to him
For her it represented the submission
She gave him and all it embodied
When she worshiped his cock
She was loving him, adoring him, and thanking him
She strived to learn
Improve her skills
Finding new ways to show her devotion
This love and appreciation was so strong

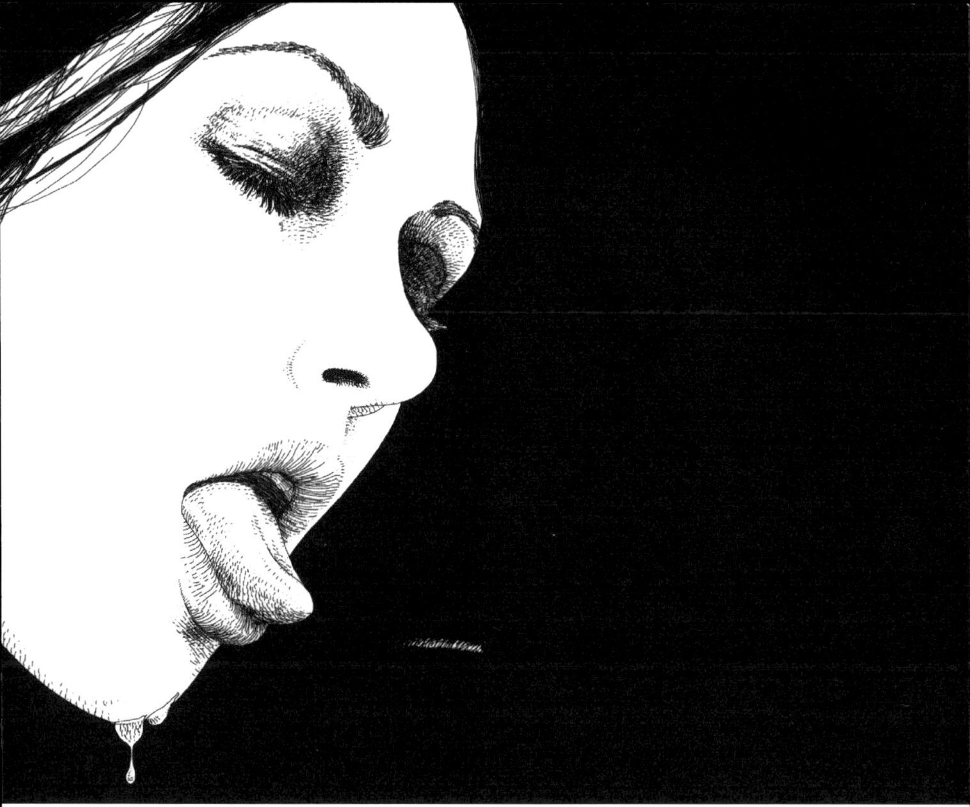

It became an aspiration of hers
To become a cock worshipping artist

She thought of running her tongue along his shaft
Taking him into her throat
Almost feeling a click in her wind pipe
As he slipped in farther
She would swallow and swallow again
Just in case she could pull him into her even more
She thought of how she wanted to caress his cock all the time
For her this was a part of her worship for his cock
Having him in her mouth was a mere portion of the act

She got up from the bed
Went down on her knees
Resting her palms up on her thighs

He too left the bed and stood in front of her
Her huge eyes looking up into his
Begging with every single blink

She said, "Sir, may I please worship your cock
Please, Sir, I need to feel you inside me
I need to show you how much you mean to me
There are no words to replace this act
Please, Sir"

Tears started to roll down her face
As she thought about the possibility
Of him denying her
It felt like a gut punch

He replied, "You may, but not until I say"

For her the anticipation of his cock
About to enter her mouth, made it water
Like a luscious meal after a long fast
That first moment his stem
Touched her lips sent her floating
She would open her mouth instinctively wider
As he slipped in
Showing her trust but also ownership
He owned her
She felt this most when he fucked her face
As hard as he could
Using her for his pleasure
Seeing what she could take
She would steal partial breaths
As to not stop the momentum for a moment
Going as long as he wanted
Every kiss, lick and drop of love drool
Was filled with reverence and exaltation
This was her religion

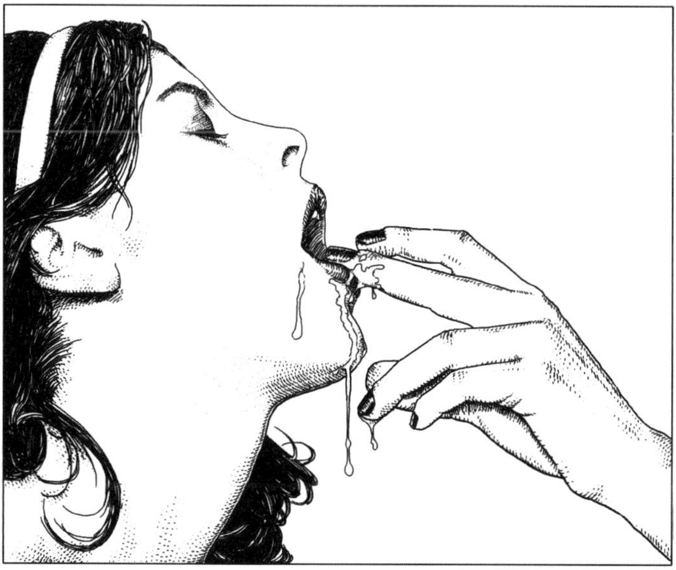

Four Course Meal

By Leaena

Appetizer:

Want and need with hints of earth and spice

Carefully crafted with the longing of a thousand nights

Served warm and willing on bended knees

Soup:

Lust thick and creamy only meant for a silver spoon

Exotic ingredients found only in the darkest mind

Served with devotion for dipping

Entrée:

Carnal Knowledge of the most tender flesh
Delectable morsels with the scent and taste of the sea
Served hot to the touch and meant to burn

Dessert:

Pleasure sweet and sticky coating everything
Syrupy lassitude permeates the limbs and mind
Served with pounding hearts and whispered sighs

No matter your riches
This is a menu for One

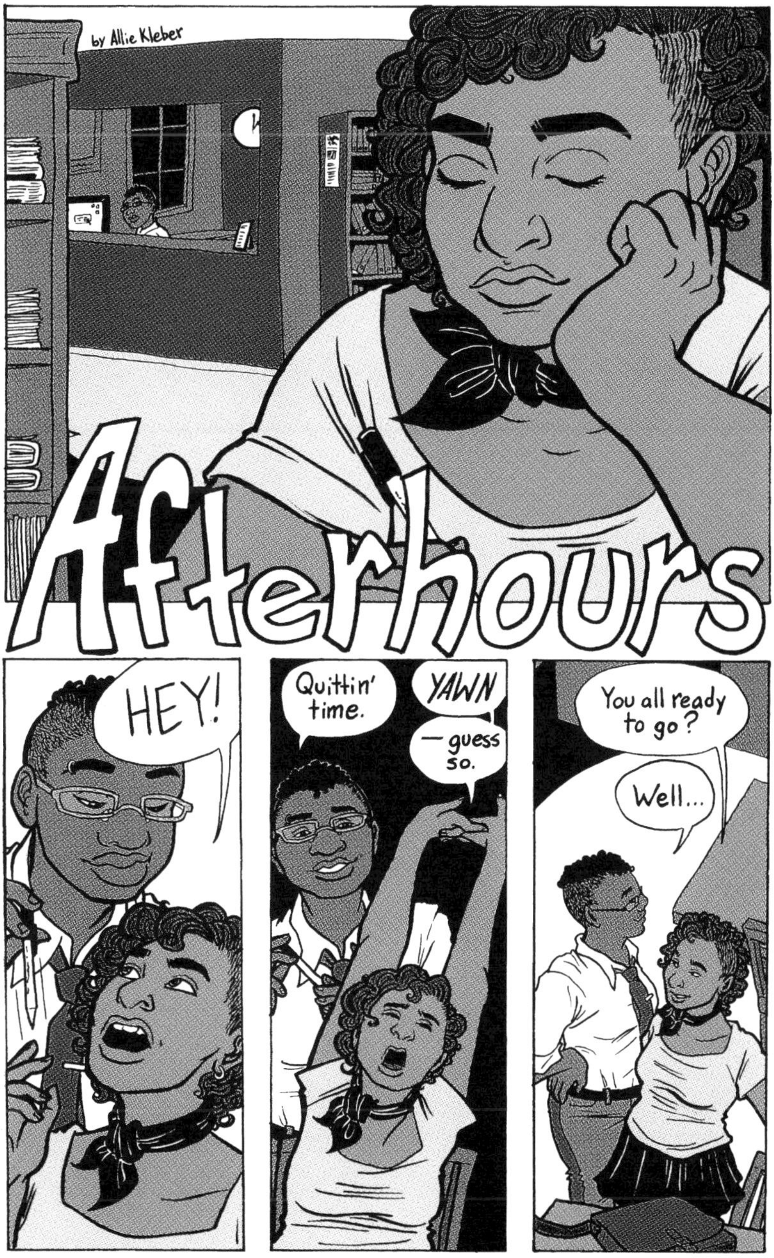

By Allie Kleber

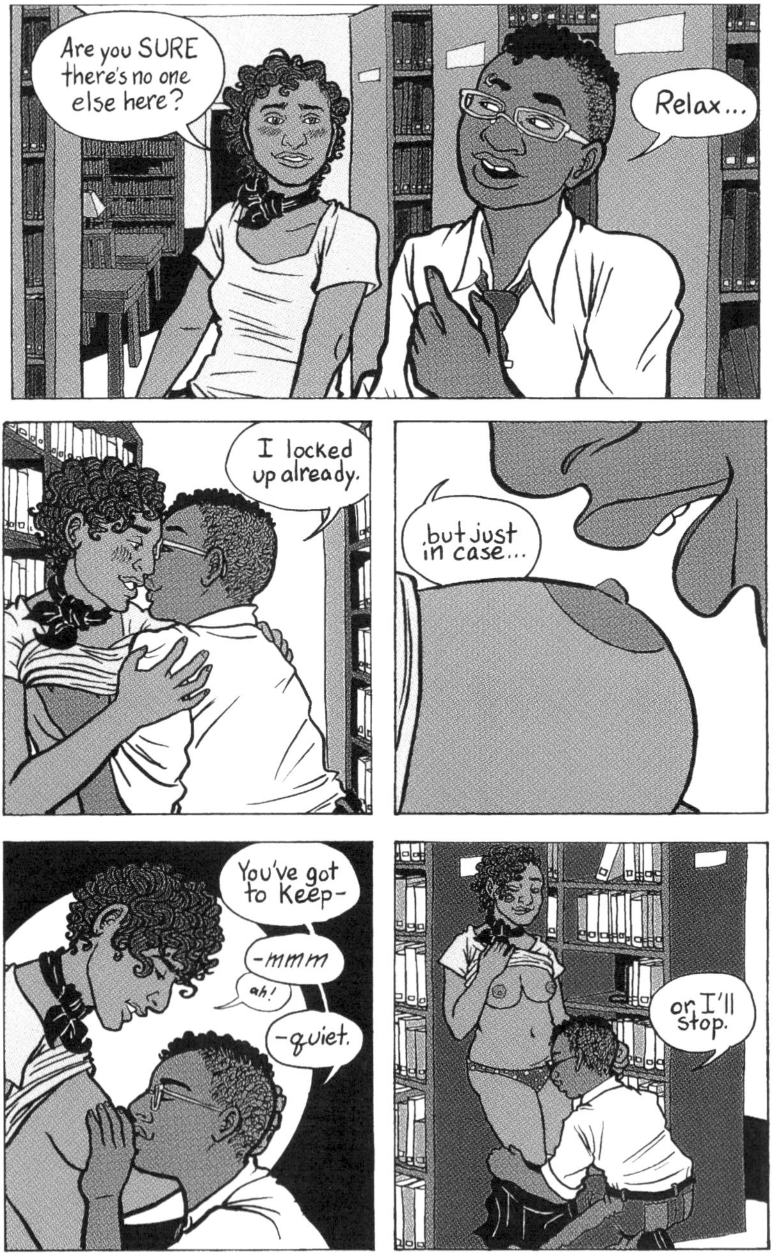
Are you SURE there's no one else here?
Relax...
I locked up already.
but just in case...
You've got to keep-
-mmm
ah!
-quiet.
or I'll stop.

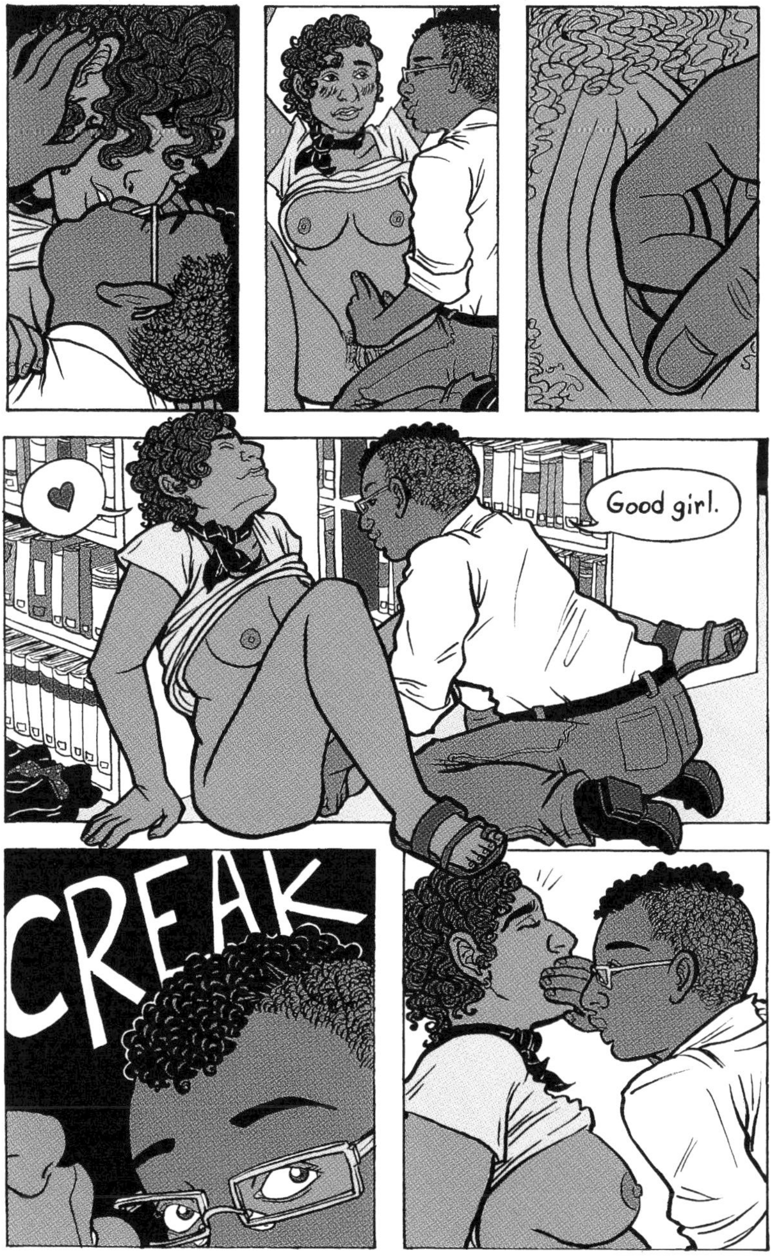
Good girl.
CREAK

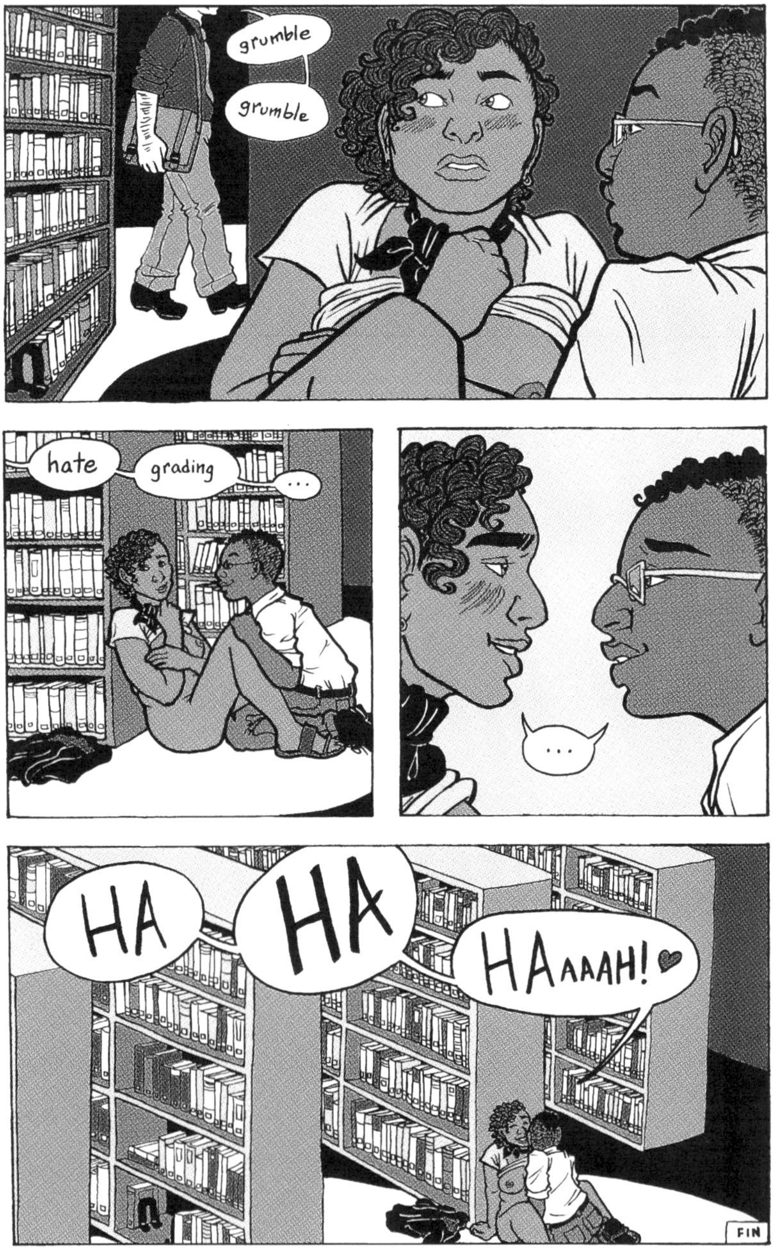
grumble
grumble
hate
grading
...
...
HA
HA
HAaaah! ♥
FIN

Trapped and Safe

By Sasha Lewis

I know I'm in trouble the second the door closes. I feel your heavy breath on the back of my neck, and I know I have to get away. I break out in a run but you are right behind me. I make it as far as the bedroom, trying to close the door behind me, but you push it open and lunge for me, grabbing a fist full of my hair as you push me toward the bed. I am panicked now, and I begin to wrestle against you, fighting to get the upper hand, but you grab both my wrists and pin me down to the bed, straddling my waist, pinning my thighs under your body weight. You look down at me and smile, lean forward and whisper in my ear that I have been very bad and that I need to be punished. I try to kick you off of my by squirming my legs underneath you, but as you hold down my wrists with one hand, the other closes around my throat and puts just enough pressure there that I know you are serious. I still my body and look up to you with alarm in my eyes, but also something else...despite myself I am excited by your rough treatment, and I am already starting to get wet between my legs...

You flip me over and hike up my dress, pressing your already hardening cock in between my ass... You cover my body with yours, pinning me down, and I can feel your pants pressing into my ass as you start moving against me... Again you whisper in my ear, "You are in trouble Sasha. I am going to hurt you. I know you want that don't you?" I don't answer you, just whimper into the sheet. You grab my hair roughly and pull my head back..."I asked you a question Sasha. Answer me."

I hesitate to answer and you grab my hair harder. "Yes, I want you to hurt me." I say, as an embarrassed blush blooms across my cheeks.

"That's what I thought," you say laughing at my embarrassment. "Now I am going to get off of you, and you are going to stay there like an obedient little girl aren't you." I nod my head yes as you lift most of your weight off of me, still pressing a firm hand in between my shoulder blades in case I try to make an escape. You rip my

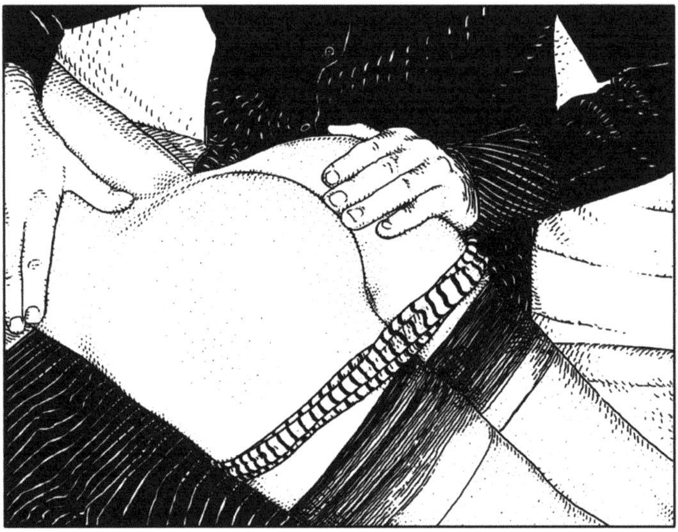

panties off of me and blow your hot breath across my ass cheeks.

“We are going to start with my hand. There will be 20. You will count them down, thank me for each one and ask me for another. Is that understood?”

“Yes,” I say a little bit breathless, already filled with anticipation. Your hand comes down hard on my bare ass, making a delicious cracking sound. “I...Thank you may I have another.”

More blows reign down, increasingly harder, my ass is heating up and the sting makes me squirm. I count them off, trying not to lose count in my head as the pain/pleasure gets more intense. I have just thanked you for the last one and still asked for another, when you forcefully stick your fingers into my hot, dripping wet pussy, pushing in and out.

You chuckle at me, “You love being punished don’t you, you slut?”

“Yes,” I say getting even more worked up with the way you fingering me. I bear down on your fingers, trying to force them deeper and you laugh at me, and I still my movements. You pull your fingers out and I feel empty without them...you then shove them into my mouth forcing me to taste my own arousal. I eagerly suck on your fingers, showing you that I am ready to suck on something else.

"Sit up on your knees," you order, "hands behind your back." I get in position as you stand up on the bed, your cock, hard from punishing me stands proudly in front of my face. I try not to drool thinking of having it in my mouth, but you look me in the eye and can see how much I want it. "You want me to fuck your face slut?" you ask and you slap me in the face with your hard cock. "Say it."

"I want you to fuck my face," I say, no longer trying to hide my obvious excitement at the prospect.

"Open up slowly," you say as you slide the tip between my lips. Your hand goes to the back of my head and then you shove your cock the rest of the way inside, hard and deep. My eyes begin to water, and saliva floods my mouth as I fight back the gag reflex.You stay deep in my throat steady for a second, then you pull back out slowly and then shove it all the way back in, hitting the back of my throat. You pick up a punishing rhythm, fucking my throat hard and deep. I struggle to keep my hands behind my back, when all I want to do is grab your ass and pull you even deeper down my throat, but for now you set the pace. I am so excited by the sounds coming out of you....your breathing is very fast and you are giving off these delicious little intoxicating moans. Your thrusting is getting more erratic and suddenly you pull completely out, turn me around and shove me onto the bed. You pull me up on my knees and in a second you are over me, pushing your hard cock deep inside of my pussy, pounding me like a man possessed. I am so wet and ready for you and I love the frantic pace. Knowing that I brought you to that place has me so excited.

"Touch yourself," you order and I start vigorously playing with my clit. I can feel the sexual energy rising between us, going higher and higher. I am close but I know not to cum until you give me permission...so I wait on the precipice...my whole body is beginning to shake. "Now," you say and and I cum hard, squeezing your cock in a hot vice like grip, as you follow me over the edge, spilling inside me. My knees give out and I collapse, bringing you down on top of me, your weight pressing in to me, making me feel trapped and safe all at the same time.

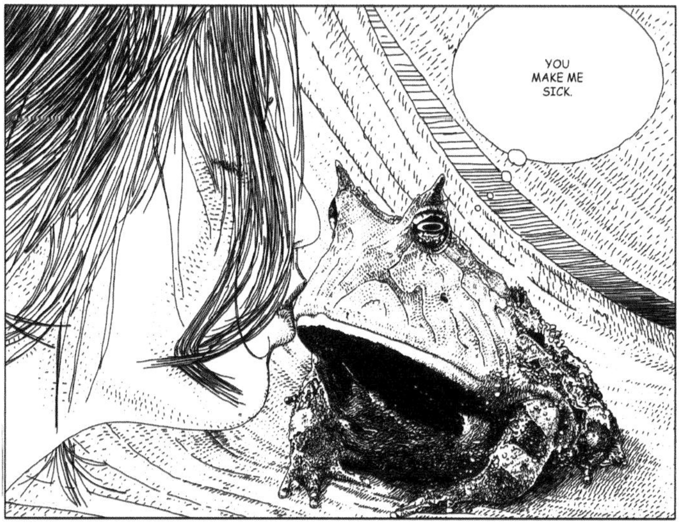

And then I became a Princess

By Nocturne Noir

Since being introduced to the BDSM lifestyle, I have been fascinated by how each role parlays into regular relationships. So many people are participating in BDSM relationships in the vanilla world, the real world and have no clue that they are. I know looking back at my life, I have been practicing one form or another of BDSM most of my adult life.

When I first joined an online site for Kinksters, within the first week I was bombarded with men wanting to "prostrate" to me. While I had some experience playing the Domina in real life play sessions this type of 24/7 submission was so foreign to me coming from a patriarchal society. I briefly found myself talking to a few trying to dissect what made them tick. Sadly, I found them mistakenly thinking of humiliating themselves for the affections of a woman.

This had no appeal to me. To be submissive is one thing, but to completely view yourself as worthless is another. Just way too much Hollywood fantasy—mainly the S/m themed advertisements, the badly made domination films, and magazines that show vicious women manhandling their compliant and appreciative submissive male(s). And much as I enjoyed very much the morbid twisted idea of WWII-style uniformed Domina from hell interrogating her male prisoners, I realized that outside of these fantasies, I didn't enjoy being a Domina. I don't like demanding obedience, and requiring compliance is not my thing. I don't enjoy pulling people my way or forcing them to do tasks.

Some time later, I met a likable fella who claimed to be a Dominant who wanted to help me disinhibit myself and explore. Well, we explored for that week.

I became the "good girl."

I LOVED TO HEAR THAT!

Those words sent my heart soaring and made me feel proud like no career achievement ever had. I couldn't believe how much joy that brought to my life the first time I heard those words. However, I was not truly a "submissive." I could not maintain my submission outside of play. Constantly questioning, prodding and challenging. My inner beee-atch came out. I can be quite a beeee-atch, yes I can. Not bratty just for the sake of causing problems, but my standards are high. I can't respect or obey someone who doesn't respect me, nor someone I don't feel deserves my respect. Respect is a *HUGE* thing for me! And yes I feel I am entitled to good treatment. I want things in a certain way. I actually demand it, even if silently. So after that was that, I knew wasn't a submissive, after all.

Then I met an intelligent chivalrous man who unexpectedly who flew into my life, challenging me, questioning me, understanding me, caring for me .... and making me feel myself in a way no one had before.

I felt cherished, treasured and honoured.

So all those roles flipped through my mind that I looked at just for amusement. I came to the full realization that I have become a PRINCESS. All my work up to this point in life, with even knowing it lead here. And it just took that one special person to realize it. I felt like a Princess. My trusted instincts told me, "This what you are. Your instincts know what you want, even if your mind or heart do not."

There's something about a princess.

When I was a little girl I sure thought so. I had a princess doll, princess dress-up clothes, even a princess tiara—you get the picture. But I wasn't that unusual. So many little girls, from so many generations, have grown up with dreams of being a princess. And what's at the center of Disney World's Fantasyland? Cinderella's Castle, of course.

But sadly, so many women have been treated like anything but royalty. They've been used, abused, battered, betrayed, excluded, abandoned, diminished – which is to say, completely and utterly undervalued. The Princess dreams go down in flames when the men around you are less than men. Or when the air-brushed images of beauty in our world make you feel anything but special.

And yet, there are many women who may never wear crowns, but who have discovered how a woman becomes a true Princess.

How did I become a Princess?

I did not become a princess by one day donning a fancy gown and a glittery tiara, then acting indulgently spoiled, pampered and audaciously entitled, having men pay me tribute by paying my bills. That is not a Princess.

The day I became a Princess (without even realizing it) was the day I decided how I wanted to be treated. And how I wanted my relationship with *my King* to be. I learned in all my 34 years that YOU teach people how to treat you. *Yesssssss, YOU!* This means that the way people treat you depends on how they react to the impression you make with your actions and visible persona, but also how you treat others.

It was up to me to decide what people said or did to me. After years of abuse and self-imposed emotional-masochism I decided I was done. In other words: the shit you receive from others directly relates to how carry yourself and how you respond to everything in life.

Instead of complaining about men (and women, too) NOT being Rhett Butler-esque, I decided to reverse the focus 180° degrees and ask myself:

Are you a lady?

I wasn't sure. But I set off myself en route to becoming a woman, a lady. Accepting my flaws, healing past hurts and being confident about my femininity. That was freedom to me. And I knew I needed to work towards it.

Then I asked myself:

Are you the best version of yourself?

Then with this awareness I started to look around the street and even the TV, only to find 6/10 women I saw were:

> Women who are monstrously uncared for and unkempt ... with no plans to change or improve themselves.
>
> Girls showing off their ignorance and lack of education with prideful attitude.
>
> Showboat-bunnies mentioning blow-jobs, their vagina and other vulgarity in every other sentence.

It begs the question:

Why would a man ever make an effort to treat such an individual with any care or respect?

Then I concluded that the dilemma is NOT about refusing to accept certain behaviour from men. Men will not change because you all of the sudden raise your standards, make new demands, start to expect more of them, and feel you deserve flowers. No, no my dear sweet lovelies they won't!

Respect needs to be earned!

The solution is teaching people how to treat you, but first and foremost changing yourself so that you, yourself deserve gratitude and admiration.

I'm not going to beat around the bush: it is simply unrealistic to expect any chivalrous acts from a Knight if you don't reflect the attributes of a Princess. I'm talking external and internal here. I needed to look my best (or least better) to please my surrounding environment.

Helena Rubinstein said once, "There are no ugly women, only lazy ones."

This might sound sexist towards my own gender, and yes, I'm sorry if it does ... But I simply do not understand women who refuse to make an effort with themselves. However, looks are't everything yes I know. Not everyone is Top Model. I know I'm not. But it's the more about the whole package darlings. I had to nurture my heart and also my mind. I did a lot of internal reflection. Reconnecting with my noble, kind, trusting, faithful, respectful, admirable and humble altruistic self. Working towards femininity. And finding the courage to allow my inner "sparkle" shine through.

I came also to the realization I AM a wicked-smart, strong-willed über-competent, synergistic crusader of life. Gone are the Princesses of the old, who sat in ivory towers waiting for their Knights to rescue them. No darlings, I'm talking about modern 21st century Princesses who are not victims or doormats. We design our own family crest (identity). We keep our own eyes for villains. We can slay our dragons. We don't let peas stay under our mattresses letting them eat us up. We accept that poisoned apples are a part of life. We know our friends are our Fairy Godmothers. We do good deeds daily. We know how to address an audience. We understand now that our carriage (or pumpkin) doesn't define us. We grasp that history is our best teacher. We're patrons of the beauty around us. We regularly present honorary awards to the people who deserve them. We treat our homes like castles and keep them running smoothly. We find our own glass slippers understanding no one size fits all. And we stand and stride straight and tall… And we dance … to our own beat—never sitting on the sidelines at the Ball.

When you are a person of class who radiates elegance and dignity, men worthy of you will learn to respect you. They will adjust their behaviour from "*Asshole*" to "*Asshole with manners*" then slowly gradually to "Gentleman." All men have the potential to quiet down their inner caveman. Men seem to be intrigued by the mystery of women with principles and want to be with women they believe are in some way "superior" to them. That's the inner caveman speaking hehe, like he conquered something marvelous!

So use your attitude and behaviour to alter his perception towards this direction. On the other hand, if you express indignity, ignorance and inelegance you will attract the same back from the man you're currently with. It's a spade for a spade.

There will be slip-ups and sometimes you will find yourself having accepted another idiot's behaviour. I know I keep doing this. It's fine, be elegant, graceful about this as life is a constant learning curve. And this is a practice of self-awareness which comes with experience and personal development. But by trying your best to honour your boundaries and intentions as they will earn you a King who will move more than one square to be with you. Sometimes you have to take personal risks and cut out that guy who refuses to accept your terms. *Tough luck Buddy!* I've thrown enough frogs back into the water to know this. A guy who doesn't respect your rules on conduct has no business in your life anyway.

And once you have the treatment you deserve, when you feel like a Princess you are able to appreciate your man, your King by returning his favours. And also treat him like the King he deserves. And as we know in the BDSM world, men and women (or even same gender) were born to serve each other in love, trust, honour, devotion and respect. Completely the yin and yang we know as a whole.

So as the song lyrics from LowKey go...

"If you don't respect yourself, no one's gonna respect you
If you don't love yourself, no one's gonna love you"

Simple Harmonic Oscillation

By Northern Star

Loud, I imagine them,
Burgundy, dark
the colour of bruised skin,
Jagged and sharp, demanding,
screaming with hunger,
The sound waves of my desire.
And then you talk,
Hushed, sweet words
That only I can hear,
Commanding me,
Lulling me into trance.
And I am riding the sound waves
Of your voice as you
connect us
All sharp edges drop away,
Clarity of sound,
There is just you
Transforming me
Sound waves large enough
to carry me, I know not where,
But I go willingly.
And now you are the ocean Orgasmic
And I am awash in you.

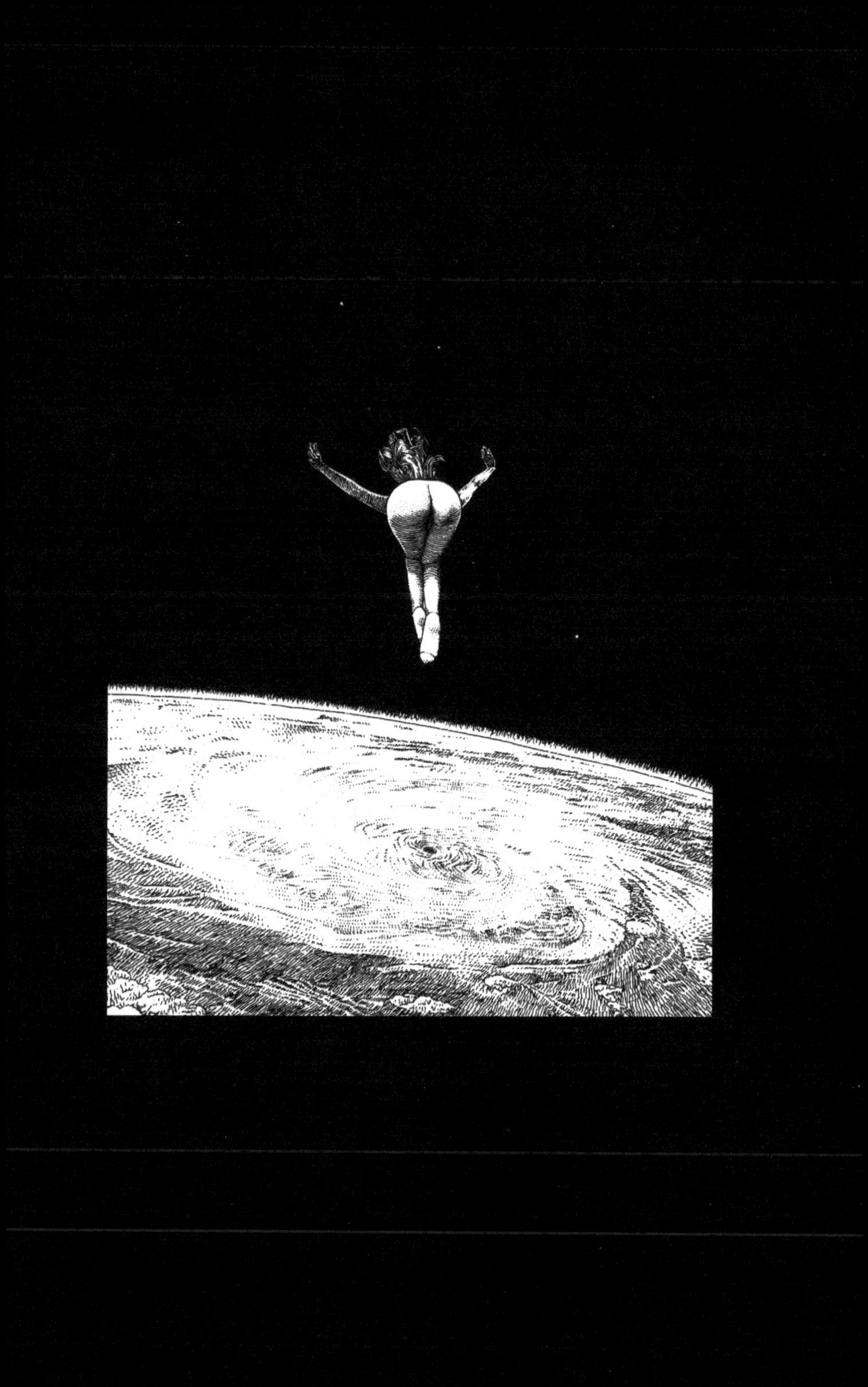

Pride of cock

By Olivia Hellbond

Let me rain down, on your mind with words of satin, my hands caress with tingles of blessing. While I stare to you with a mouth of your pride. Sucking with want and love, licking from base to sack. Milking him of his strength. To swallow with excitement that brings a euphoria of her own.

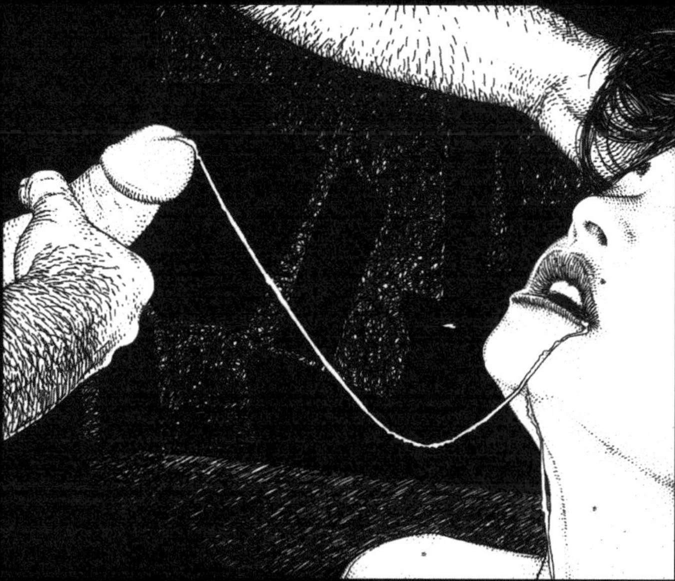

Sweet Dreams Are Made of This

By Northern Star

Empowered and energized
by your responses
I take ownership of your pleasure
and play you,
slow sensuous concerto of tongue,
staccato percussion of fingers
that hold your balls firmly,
squeezing, pleasure pain,
then slide rhythmically to stroke
backward towards puckered bud
that wishes also to play along,
tempo of your swollen cock
holding steady in the rhythmic strokes
of my tongue,
your laboured breath and
moans and sighs of
nonsense words and pleas,
a perfect lyrical harmony
to the symphony I play

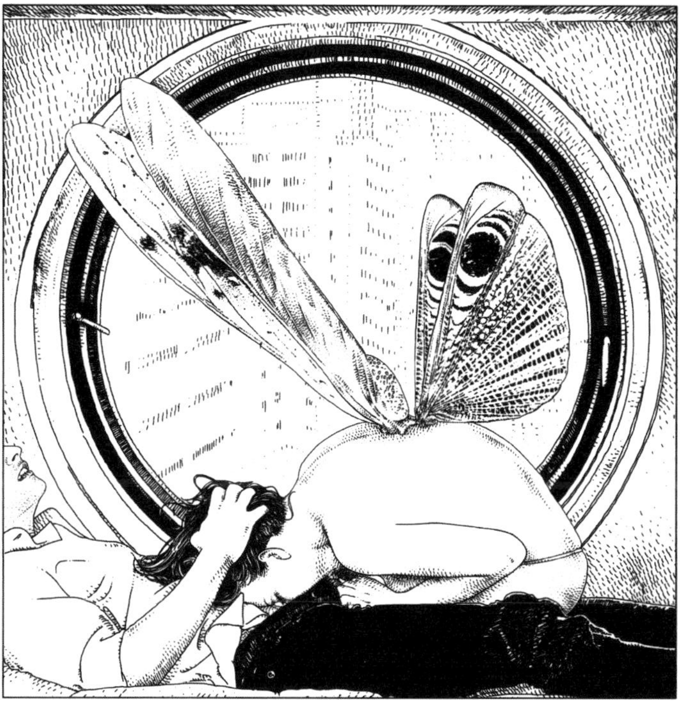

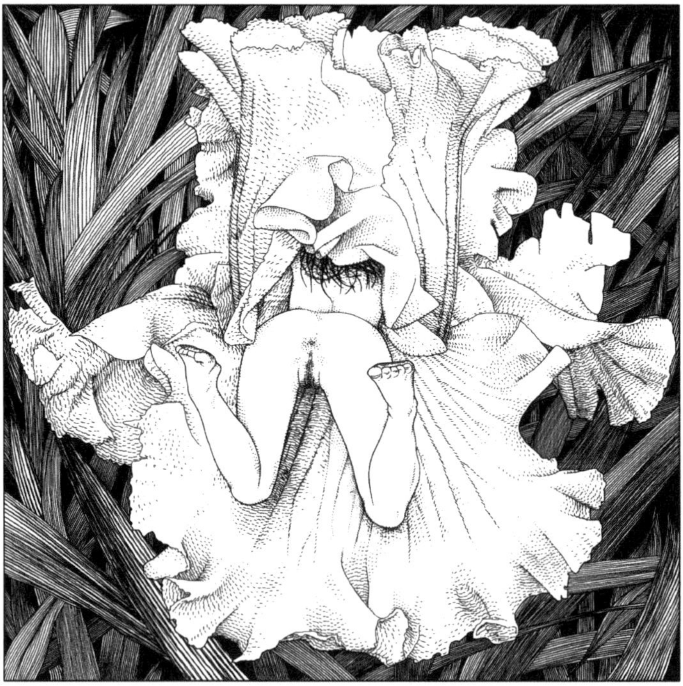

poetry of your skin

By Nocturne Noir

The poetry of your skin
Is written with
Dangerous threshed curvatures,
Deep trenched creases,
And satiny glabrous skin,
All that laminar flowing flesh
That reminds me of a warm late-Autumn day.
Your perfume invades
My senses
Smothers my thoughts

And then takes me away...
I dream...
I stretch ..
I play...
Sweet touch,
Sweet kiss,
Sweet secret
Between you and me.
Oh my dearest!
Touch me again,
Touch me
Where life is an eclipsed metaphor
And oceans cross frontiers,
Touch me there ...
The poetry of your skin
Reveals ...
Exposes ...
Conceals ...
Surrounds ...
I'm in love
In awe
With the way
Your body wears my name
On your lips
In between kisses
Contesting you are mine.
Lolling on you like a necklace
Still wet from your smoldering kiss.
You smear my insides
With your tension
Manipulation
And percussion.
Nothing else could be more beautiful than these
Delicate moments of delightful debauchery ...
And nothing else is more sinfully intense
Than this
Poetry of your skin.

New Passions

By Eleanor Regan

'More wine?'

I knew the line tonight between a bit tipsy and far too drunk couldn't be blurred, but after spending time enjoying her company, I was running out of reasons not to just take her right there on my sofa. I would plan a gentle but passionate move as I drank my wine, instead of a frenzied and passionate pounce.

'Yes.'

She answered so quickly, her voice laced with anticipation and nerves.

'Sorry, yes please, that would be lovely.'

As I took her glass from her, we locked eyes. They seemed to speak a thousand silent words with just a single glance. They were entirely arousing. She looked at me wide-eyed, eyes so blue it made me think she held the world's oceans within her. An ironic thought, considering as I looked at her all I could feel in myself was a burning fire of want.

As I sat beside her, close enough to touch, I could see the rise and fall of her chest, her breathing increasingly rapid as time went by, a combination of nerves and excitement. I very much intended to make her forget all about her nerves. She held an empty wine glass in her hand, as if it were a safety blanket, perhaps unsure as to what she would do with that hand if it were free.

I leant across her to take the glass from her and place it down on the table. As I did so my lips brushed the soft skin of her shoulder. A small gasp followed by a very quiet 'oh my' sent sparks of arousal direct to my pussy. Want had turned to need. A need that was begging to rip her clothes off, and take her right there with a rough and fiery passion. But I had promised to be gentle and patient, which I could do. For a little while at least.

My lips left a trail of kisses from shoulder to mouth, as I placed my hand on her knee and slowly slid up her thigh, teasing myself as much as her. It stopped short of her pussy, I could feel the heat of her radiating through her jeans. As I kissed her, her tongue gently dancing with my own, my mind swirled with thoughts of how wet she would be. I wanted her to drip for me, to come for me, I wanted her to beg for more, I wanted to make her come until she begged me to stop, and if she asked nicely, I might.

How I managed to pull my lips from hers is beyond me. Her desire was rising through her body and spilling from her tongue to mine. It was addictive, but I needed more of her. As I pulled away her eyes stayed closed, her lips still parted ever so slightly, glistening with moisture from our kiss; her breasts encased in a beautiful corset, so beautiful I was tempted to leave it on; but the desire to have her naked before me would win.

I put my mouth to her ear, trying to find words slightly more poetic than 'I want to fuck you' but none came, so I simply took her hand and said 'Come with me'.

As we reached the bed I sat down and pulled her to me so she stood between my legs. Turning her around I started to undo her corset, my hands trembling with the urge to go faster, but I knew the anticipation would be making her arousal grow as it was mine. This was one occasion where patience truly was a virtue. Finally the corset fell to the floor. Her back was still to me, and my hands travelled across her stomach, then moved upwards to cup her breasts as my mouth kissed and tongue flicked across the base of her back, travelling up her spine, until I reached her neck, my hands enthralled by the contrast between the gentle curves of her breasts and the hard arousal of her nipples, my self-control waivering, and my teeth forgot my promise to be gentle as they slowly but firmly bit into her flesh. There was a sharp intake of breath, followed by the unmistakable 'oh fuck' of an aroused woman, and I knew then the gentle line had moved ever so slightly.

I sat back down on the bed and started to run my hands across the fabric of her jeans. This time there was no stopping. My hands flowed across her thighs, her arse, then I cupped what I knew would be a hot, wet pussy underneath her clothes and pulled her closer to to me.

'Turn around.'

My heart pounded with excitement as she responded, my pussy twitching with the desire to ask more of her. Once again I reminded myself there was no rush, I had time to enjoy her, to savour her, every touch, every taste would be delicious, so it was hard not to want it all at once. I started to unbuckle her jeans, the thrill of revealing her completely coursing through me. My mind was suddenly lost in thought of how this was the body, the woman who had caused her own orgasm to my words, how I had made her come with messages of all I wanted to do to her. I wanted to see how that looked. In that moment I was consumed by the desire to see her pleasure herself and having her there had me in the mood to get just what I wanted.

I hadn't been wrong; once her jeans were removed I could feel how wet her knickers were, soaked right through,; I wanted to see her fingers coated in her own wetness, then I wanted to remove them, lick them and replace them with my own so I could feel her pussy spasm and clench as I made her come. I wanted a lot: all I had done was want her, from the moment I realised how hot fucking her would be.

I removed her underwear, and the sight of her pussy sent a ripple of pure lust right through me. My mind was set though, I'd have to wait. We switched positions, so she was sat on the bed, totally and wonderfully naked and I stood before her fully clothed. I leant down to kiss her and ease her down so she was lying in the bed. My fingers had a brief but exquisite encounter with her pussy, while I found out whether I could get what I wanted.

'Remember how you fingered yourself until you came, while I sent you all those naughty messages?'

'Yes ... of course.'

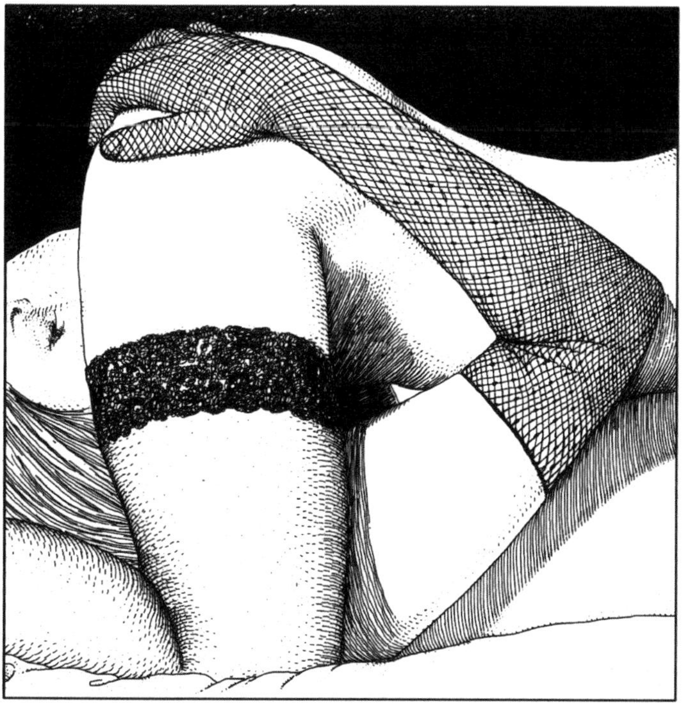

'I want you to do that for me now, so I can watch as I undress.' Her closed eyes suddenly flew open, those big blue eyes suddenly nervous again. I remember being filled with reluctance when a lover had asked me to do this. Now I wasn't sure I'd ever refuse again. I suddenly understood how arousing it could be. I needed her to understand too. My fingers still playing and exploring, I tried to find the words of encouragement needed.

'I have pictured that scene in my mind, over and over, I have touched myself to those images. They make me wet and horny, and they make me want to fuck you, like I do now. I want to do it right though, show me how you like to be touched, so I can learn from it and make you come again and again. Start now. While my hand is there too and keep going until I take over. I promise it will be worth it.'

Ever so slowly, her hand moved. I felt her fingers as they hesitantly laced into my own inside her.

'That's it. Perfect. Remember don't stop. Just fuck.'

And she did. Her hips started to move, her breathing became rapid, her bottom lip caught between her teeth until a small moan escaped, a moan that told me an orgasm was building, I wanted that orgasm, I wanted it clenched around my fingers as she pushed onto them, finding the pleasure she wanted. I lay my body down beside hers, the heat radiating from her body reaching my own. My hand slid down to meet hers, as I pulled her fingers away, there was a little moan of complaint, no woman enjoys having her pleasure interrupted, I knew she would forgive me once I'd made her come. First though I sucked her fingers into my mouth and licked them clean.

'You taste amazing.' My fingers were back inside her pussy, imitating the moves she had made with her own.

'I'm going to taste you as you come for me later; right now though, my fingers get the pleasure.'

'Fuck ... Yes ... Oh yes ...'

With that last 'yes' her pussy gripped my fingers, and her body was gripped by orgasm. I couldn't take my eyes off her. A woman in the throes of passion is truly a beautiful thing.

As she lay there, her breathing gradually returning to something like normal, my mouth decided that had to change. Once my lips locked on hers, the post-orgasm calm that had washed over her gave way to passion, her hand found her way into my hair, forming a fist, and slowly but firmly she pulled, our lips forced apart.

'Remember how I was nervous and you promised to be gentle and patient?'

'Yes, of course.'

'Did I promise you the same?'

'Not at all.'

'Good.'

With that everything changed. Any control I had started to slip away. My brief triumph was just that: brief. Her eyes shone with a wickedness that I was eager to explore. I was helpless to resist. Part of me wanted to, part of me wanted to try, but I couldn't resist her. I wanted her so much, I wanted her to be wet and wanting and full of desire and I would do whatever I had to do to get her there.

She pulled my mouth back to hers and kissed me, her soft lips voicing a fierce passion. Her weight slowly shifted so I was pinned beneath her. I felt her mouth against my ear, her voice a quiet whisper, but laced with a desire that made my pussy throb.

'I want you...'

'Oh god ... I want you too.'

She let out a small chuckle that threw me completely. It was sexy as hell, but I had no clue as to what I had done to cause it. Luckily an explanation came before I needed to ask.

'As pleased as I am to hear that, I hadn't finished my sentence. What I was saying was, I want you... to behave.'

That was it, I was done, I had no desire to be in control, I wanted to behave, I wanted to find out what my reward would be if I was good for her. Time lost all meaning while her hands ran over my body, every inch explored, her lips alternating between my mouth, my neck, my nipples, leaving me writhing with desire beneath her, desperate for more.

'You make it very hard to play with you. You are a very wriggly little toy. So, stay still.'

With every ounce of control I had I stayed still. In my mind I'd done it, not a muscles was moved. It was hard. Her fingers moving in and out of me, slowly, quickly, somehow finding their way to that perfect spot inside me, ever so gradually pushing me closer and closer to climax. It wouldn't take much to push me over the edge.

'Turn over. Then stay. Still.'

The change in position had pulled me back from the edge, ever so slightly. Her fingers though, oh my, they got me there again so quickly. Just as I was thinking how I would love to push down onto her, to push myself into that orgasm, she placed a firm, strong slap on my arse. It stung, it hurt and it catapulted me right into an amazing orgasm. As I lay there my body content and tingling, I felt her hand snaking up my back, her fingers once more lacing their way into my hair, then she pulled. I couldn't stop the small moan that escaped my mouth. Her grip did not loosen as her low whisper tickled my ear.

'Did you come because I spanked you?'

'Well your fingers did the hard work, but the spanking pushed me over the edge.'

'I spanked you because you kept moving, it was a reminder to stay still.'

'Oh.'

'Oh? I punish you and all you can say is oh? I also rather get the feeling you are aroused by me pulling your hair. Am I right in thinking you really get off on the pain?'

'Yes. Very much so.'

It was true. Every spank. Every swipe of a crop. Every flogging. Every bite. Every scratch. Every pull of hair made my pussy so wet and so aroused: I didn't know how or why, but I knew it was hot as fuck when my arse radiated with the warmth of a decent beating.

‘If you are going to misbehave, and moving when told not to is definitely misbehaving, then I will have to punish you. Seeing as you love the pain so much, I think that will be your reward. If you are good, then I will beat your lovely arse, until it’s a perfect shade of red. If you are bad, no beating. Not even a single spank.’

‘I ... I was sure I didn’t move.’

‘You did. A lot. Try again, harder. Don’t move.’

She made it so hard for me, her fingers, her tongue, relentless on my pussy. I wanted to grind, and fuck, and rock, and grab, and wriggle. The need and passion coursing through my body made it almost impossible to stay still, but just as I thought I was going to give in, that I would would just convulse with desire, she spoke. Her voice still a soft whisper, but laced with the controlled desire that I was fast becoming a fan of.

‘Good girl. I knew you could it. Now come for me, and feel free to move.’

With permission granted, my body gave way, ripple after ripple coursing through me, I could feel my pussy dripping, clenching and pulsing. It was a strong, amazing orgasm, delivered by a strong, amazing woman and I was totally hooked. I knew there was a reward to be claimed, on top of an amazing orgasm that really was a wonderful thing.

I awoke the next day with an arse so sore I couldn’t sit down without a sharp intake of breath, but a beating that beautiful deserves a story all of its own.

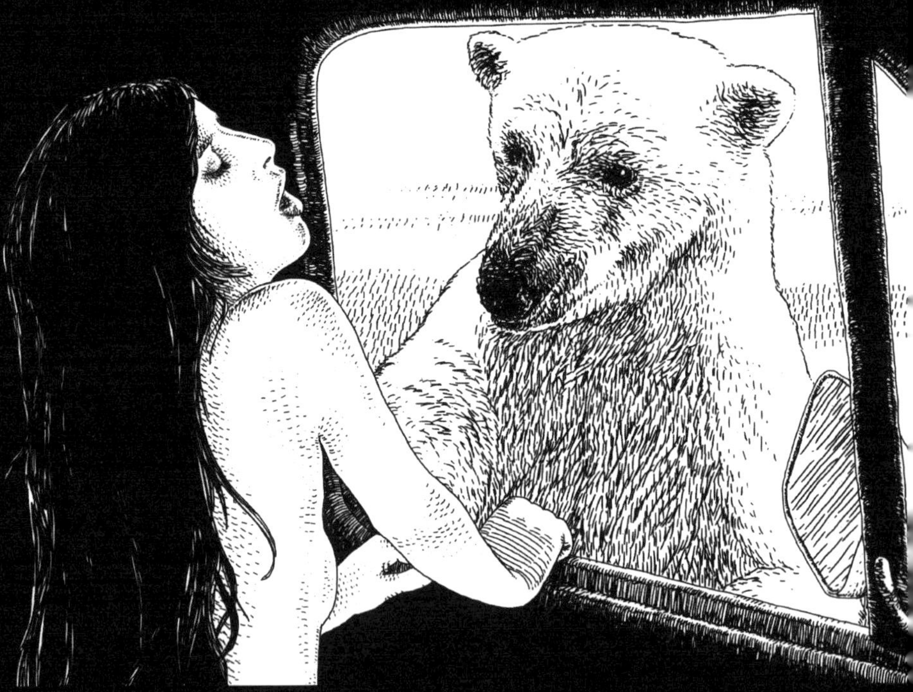

When I was a Bear

By Tori Chatfield

Before my energies
Wove a human skin
The cover they chose was fur
Claws, not fingers,
Were appendages of choice
Teeth and jaws
Could rend and savage,
And rip – no niceties or napkins
Pure clean air...snout to the wind
And raging, roaring freedom

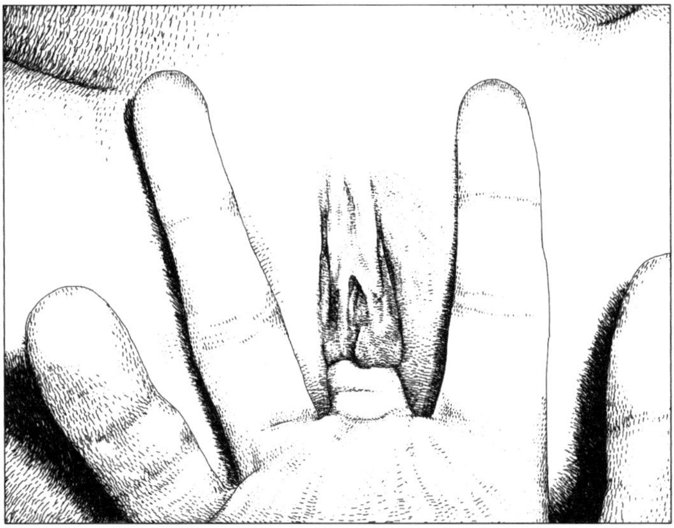

Some Like it Hotter

By Sorsha Rose

Juniper wears blond bombshell like she was born that way, scarlet siren lips, and a purposefully placed birthmark. Donning a black dress, that accentuates her ample assets: she enters the hotel.

Juniper rides the elevator up to the 18th floor. Walking down the hall and knocking on 1816. Sir opens the door but no one is there. The scent of her envelops him. He reaches his hand around the door frame and pulls Juniper into the room. Sir closes the door, pushing her roughly against it. With his hand firmly on her throat he squeezes. Then standing back, he takes in Juniper's scenic view."What took you so long?" he asks.

"It's not how long it takes, it's who's taking you," she says in her best Marilyn Monroe.
Sir sits on the bed and says,

"Clothes off."

Juniper disrobes, leaving an ebony puddle of fabric on the floor. He gets up, and pulls her to him. His soft, slightly open lips, press hers with a hefty heat she cannot deny.

He says, "This is your last chance, you can leave if you like."

She replies with that Marilyn lilt, "I don't want to go anywhere, Sir. I'm tired of getting the fuzzy end of the lollipop."

Sir inquires with a chuckle, "Are you going to talk like this all night?"

With a twinkle in her eye and the icon's voice, she says, "Whatever can you mean, Sir?"

"Would you like a spanking?" He asks.

"Oh yes, please. Thank you ever so!" Juniper replies.

Sir sits in a chair he placed perfectly earlier. He pulls her onto his lap. Her dainty fingertips touch the floor. Sir rubs her ass. Perhaps to wish her luck? He slaps her ass. Juniper moans. It's like coming home for both of them. The next swat is harder, but exquisite in its execution. Then the hits come fast and fierce. Her breathing changes. Juniper's thoughts disappear like invisible ink in a mystery novel. It hurts but what's a little hurt to the pleasure she is praying will follow?

Sir checks to see if she is wet. Her thighs are thick with a sweet nectar he can smell. The touch of his fingers on her blissful bits sends her floating out of her body. Sir keeps a finger inside her and resumes his onslaught. He thinks an ass as red as her lips would really be something to admire. He senses she is at her edge. Rubs her ass lovingly. Lifts her onto his lap and cradles her there, with her head on his shoulder. Juniper looks into his eyes, as tears escape her own. Sir smiles at her and she smiles back.

"How are you?" Sir asks.

Juniper answers, "I feel like a warm red autumn, how about you?"

Sir replies, "I want your attention. If you're smart you will get on your knees."

"I can be smart when it's important, but most men don't like it," Juniper says.

"I love that you're smart, and I love that your mine," He says

"Yes, Sir. I am yours," Juniper agrees, as she kneels on the floor; her mouth just slightly open in anticipation.

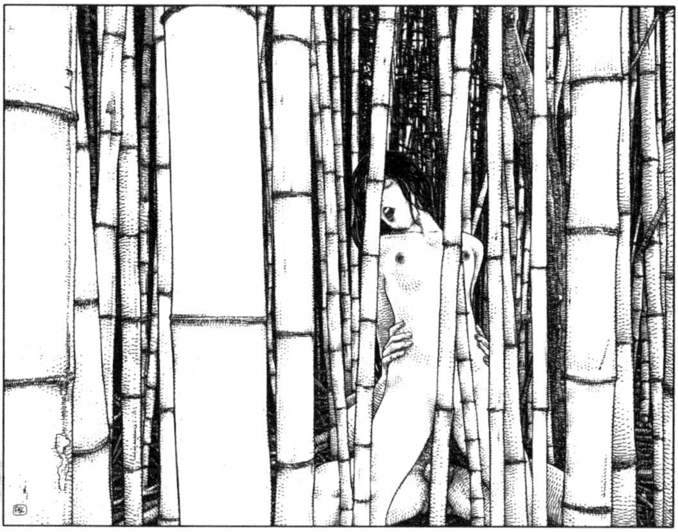

nothing else matters

By Nocturne Noir

Go softly.
Let me bathe in the river of your seduction
Dip my feet in the waters of your sin
Cast your nets in my undulating waves
Of all things unspoken
And draw in our pleasures,
Desires liquefied.
Breathe low
My soft moan stretches
Louder still until
Hoarse piercing breaths
Hang in the drenched air above
Our desirous bodies.
Envelop me
In an agony of nectarous passion,
Distilled sweet perfume of sheets,
Anguish and defeat.
The slowness of not so innocent things.
Your hands burn me, imminently.
Your mouth let it seek me out
Anchor me before I fall
Bury your mouth in mine
Letting me breathe, just breathe.
Let your tongue learn my anatomical textures,
All the shapes of my secrets.
Elude me to the point of madness,
And then offer no surrender.
Your hand creep under my gown,
Pushing your body into mine,
Sliding your puncturing lance of love
Into place.
Teach me this raw, quivering imagery.

All sweet upheaving contact,
A perfection of collarbones,
Never enough, insatiable,
Bombard me, straight to the heartbeat.
Let me taste your whirling bedlam always.
My cries tearing holes in the sound barrier
Crashing into your soul
The rhythm of your hips
That match the cadence of your words
The percussion of our sighs
And the fingers poised for the kill.
Savage violence and surrendered love
Placid sweetness and obsessive sex
Promises and betrayals.
Make me yours, be willing to draw more
From me as I take you continuously
Into the pink palaces inside me.
And in that interfused melding
That feverish molten changing
Of body for body, soul for soul
Reach deeper into the abyss of both of us
Knowing we will never fathom
What we discover.
Be-cumming
our maniacal chaos
If not
Our liberating salvation
Of unruly obsessions.
We now know nothing else matters.

Music maker

By Northern Star

Reaching out to touch you,
finger tips grazing across your arm
as your hands send
beautiful shivers through me,
electric warm and sensuous
Closing my eyes,
the better to focus on the
sensation of tongue and lips
creating madness,
mad lust,
aching hungry needy want.
Shaking, weakened,
Surrendering to your control,
All nerve endings alive only to you
Take all, it's yours
to play as you will,
Sweet songs in the chord of Oh

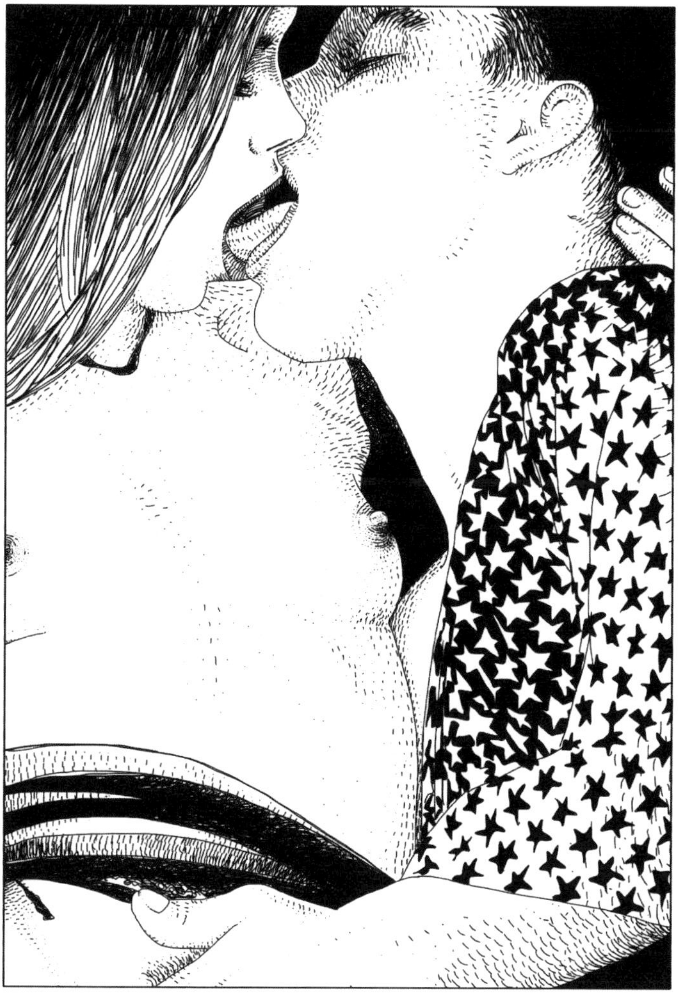

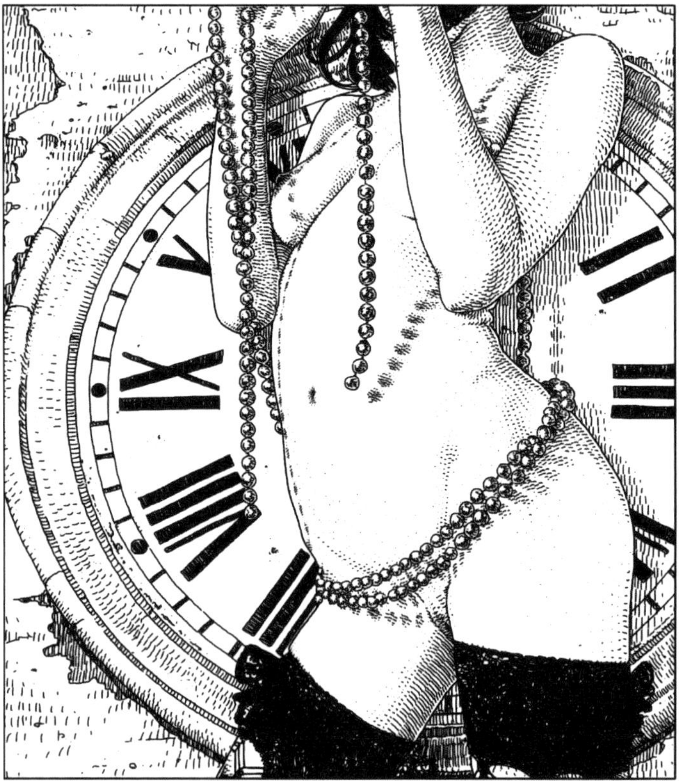

Time

By isobella

She devils the night away
puts away her display
of angel prim and proper days
7am the day begins
all housewife like
trouble and strife
you know the usual

polishing, hoovering
changing the beds
yawns whilst making a cup
of tea at 11am
One o clock
lunch time brings
feeding the kids
spam and chips
swings her large hips
washes the dish/es
listening to the news
debate, same old
3pm time for coffee
can't wait to see later on
8pm evening drags
not much on the box
restless waiting to let
down her locks
night time comes
to bed with the chores
darkness falls
11pm the spell begins
other side calls
time for whores
to let down the walls
of pretend

Taking Control

By Sasha Lewis

When I walk back into the room, you are on your knees, hands tied behind your back just where I left you. I took my time getting ready, after I bound you, leaving you to think about what a filthy, dirty man you've been, taking too much pleasure in punishing others with your cane and your brutal fucking. It is time you got a taste of your own medicine.

You look partially amused, a half smirk on your face, wondering if I have it in me to do this. Your cockiness steels my resolve and I know I have to take control of the situation. I grab your hair and pull your neck all the way back to the point where it is painful. With my other hand I caress your cheek with my fingertips. "Do you know why you are being punished Dirk?" I ask. You stare into my eyes defiantly and don't answer. The slap hits you across the face with more force than you expect and your head snaps back, and you look at me with a grin. The next slap across the other cheek is even harder, then two more in quick succession. You look me in the eye, but the smirk is gone. "Answer my question now," I say with steel in my voice and I hold your face steady, ready to slap you again if you disobey. "I am not sure," you say honestly, "it can be so many things."

I drag you to your feet and throw you face down on to the bed, hands still bound behind your back. I walk over to the side of the bed and grab a cane, hitting it against my hand as I loom over you. "Does this jog your memory?" The first hit comes down hard across your ass and you let out a loud hiss. "Repeat after me Dirk," I say as I let another blow fall across your ass. "I am a filthy, dirty man." As you repeat my words, I strike you twice more, this time a little bit lower on your thighs. I can tell you are getting excited and I can see you are starting to rut against the bed sheet looking for friction on your hard cock. "I take too much pleasure in punishing others."

"Say it," I bark when you hesitate. Four more blows come down in quick succession. Your creamy white ass is already starting to bruise. "I take too much pleasure in punishing others," you repeat. "Good boy," I say and caress your burning ass with my cool hand. I can hear your breath hitch, and you continue to rub your hardening cock against the sheets. Grabbing your ass cheeks, I pinch as hard as I can, right where it is reddest and you let out a yelp. I reach between your legs and grab your balls roughly, giving them a harsh tug and squeeze. "Still yourself now, and don't even think about coming before I give you permission," I say as I grab your balls tighter.

Grabbing you by your bound arms, I pull you up and put you on your back. I take my panties off and then climb on the bed on top of you, and sit on your face, pressing you down on the bed, onto your bound arms, not caring if it hurts. I lock my knees around your face, and push my pussy down into your mouth. "Tongue my clit now," I order. "Taste how excited I got from punishing you." Your tongue works wonders on my clit, and then I shift to push it into my opening. I am very wet and excited, and my juices flow all over your face. I ride your face harder and harder, my orgasm builds and I cum all over your face. Once the aftershocks have passed, I lift up off of your face and straddle your waist, kissing you, wanting to taste myself on your lips.

Your cock is rock hard, your breathing harsh, and your face is still painted with my release. You look amazing.

"You have pleased me, boy," I say, "And now I am going to reward you. Open your mouth," I stick three fingers inside your mouth. "Suck on them. Get them nice and wet for me." You start sucking on them in earnest, as I push them in and out of your mouth, sometimes sticking them in far, almost gagging you. When they are nice and wet, I pull them out of your mouth and I move further down your body till I have access to your ass cheeks. I circle around your hole before roughly shoving one inside. You let out a growl, but then stay still. I piston my finger in and out of your asshole, quickly adding another, to really stretch you out, scissoring them to open you up. Your legs are spread open obscenely and you are squirming under me ...moans of pain/pleasure coming out of your mouth that are driving me crazy. Having you splayed out before me, at my mercy is doing things to me. Your cock is impossibly hard now, but I still choose to ignore it, instead I push my fingers upwards and find

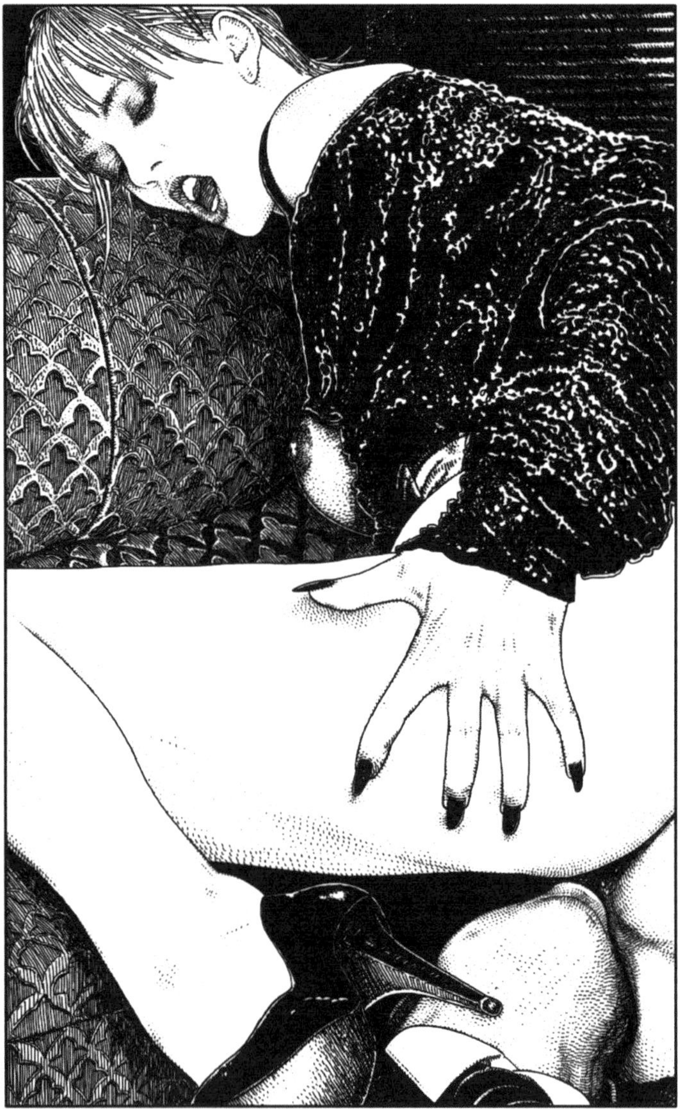

your prostate and I start pressing against it roughly, the sounds you are making now, are making me even more wet between my legs, and I know I have to taste you there. I pull your knees up higher so I have proper access and I begin by licking you around my fingers, still hitting you deep inside while also running my tongue around your hole. I pull my fingers out and then take turns lapping at it then blowing on it, as it flexes under my ministrations.

When I feel you begin to relax, I stick my tongue in and out, pistoning inside, fucking you with my tongue. You start moaning in pleasure and pushing up, wanting so bad to gain friction on your cock. I slap your cock and roughly grab your balls again and still your motion. “Do not cum,” I say, “You are my toy to play with until I am bored, and then—if you are good for me, give me pleasure—then maybe I will let you cum.” I grab your balls even tighter and slap your dick again as it bobs nice and hard in front of me. I continue to tongue your asshole till I am dripping wet with arousal and ready to move on to the next part of my plan.

Going to the night table drawer I take out a double sided dildo, one of the ones specially fitted to be inside me while I penetrate you. “Open your mouth, slut,” I say, and I place the dildo between your lips. “I want to see how pretty you would look swallowing down a cock.”

I begin to gently fuck your mouth with the dildo, enjoying the way your lips are spread around it. Popping it out of your mouth, I make sure you watch as I put the side soaked with your saliva into my pussy. You look at me with a hunger in your eyes, and my pussy clenches tightly around the dildo. “Open your mouth again,” I say as I get on the bed, one end of the dildo nestled inside me and the other waiting at your lips to be sucked on. You open up and I slip the tip of the dildo inside. You look beautiful sucking cock, tears at the corner of your eyes, as I push further and further inside. Just as you are about to gag, I pull out, get up and turn you around again, making sure your ass is in the air and ready to take a pounding. I move down the bed, and begin rimming you again, really getting you wet with saliva, opening you up with my tongue, getting you ready, so it doesn’t hurt too much.

"Please," you beg me at last. "Please fuck me, Mistress. I need it. I want it," you moan almost incoherently. "Since you begged so nicely," I say and I pull out my tongue and position myself at your entrance. Slowly I push in, hitting some resistance along the way, but I push past it. You are relaxed from the rimming, so it goes in easier. Finally I bottom out, the dildo all the way inside both of us, and the feeling is amazing. Squeezing it firmly inside of myself I pull almost completely out of your hole and then shove it back in. I set a brutally fast rhythm, taking my pleasure out of your ass. You are loving it, writhing beneath me like a common whore, moaning loudly as I pound you over and over again. The dildo is working itself inside me too, and my second orgasm is coming closer and closer. I reach around to your ignored cock, and I start jacking it off to the rhythm we are fucking. "When you are ready, I give you permission to cum." The sexual energy is building and then suddenly my orgasm washes over me like a tidal wave, and I give one last hard thrust inside you, roughly jacking your cock and you explode all over my hands. I collapse on top of you, pushing you to the bed, and stay there. After a few moments, I pull out of you slowly and pull you up to a sitting position. "I want you to clean every drop of cum off of my hand," I order and push my hand towards your mouth. Your tongue comes out and laps up every last drop. I untie your hands, and massage your wrists to get circulation back in them. I grab your face and kiss you hard, so I can taste you. "I'm beginning to see why you enjoy punishing people so much," I say with a smile. "You can punish me anytime, Mistress," you say.

Grinding To Your Melody

By Sorsha Rose

I am awoken
By the soft lull
Of the piano
It is your song you play
I step softly
See you naked
Seated on the bench
I come up behind you
Run my hands along your back
Shoulders
And arms
I press my chest into you
From behind
I get on my knees
Careful of the peddles
Staying to the side of you
I place you in my mouth
No hands
Sucking softly
Swallowing fully
You grow inside my throat
I keep on like this for a long time
You continue to play
Sucking in air between your teeth
When I take you particularly deep
I then slide myself through
Your limbs and busy fingers
I wrap my arms around
The back of your neck
I straddle you
You are already hard
Rubbing my wet against you

My body moving against yours
As I press into you
Grinding to your melody
I think I hear what might be
Missing notes
I laugh a little
You continue to play
While I keep up my tease
But you are not bound to the music
Not held by anything
Unlike me
As your hand grips my throat
You push me up onto the keys
The sound of incongruent chords
Have their own sweet tune
You enter me with ease
Until you are fully inside
Whispering lyrics in my ear
Of how you will hurt me
So tenderly
Pushing us both over the edge
This is our favorite song

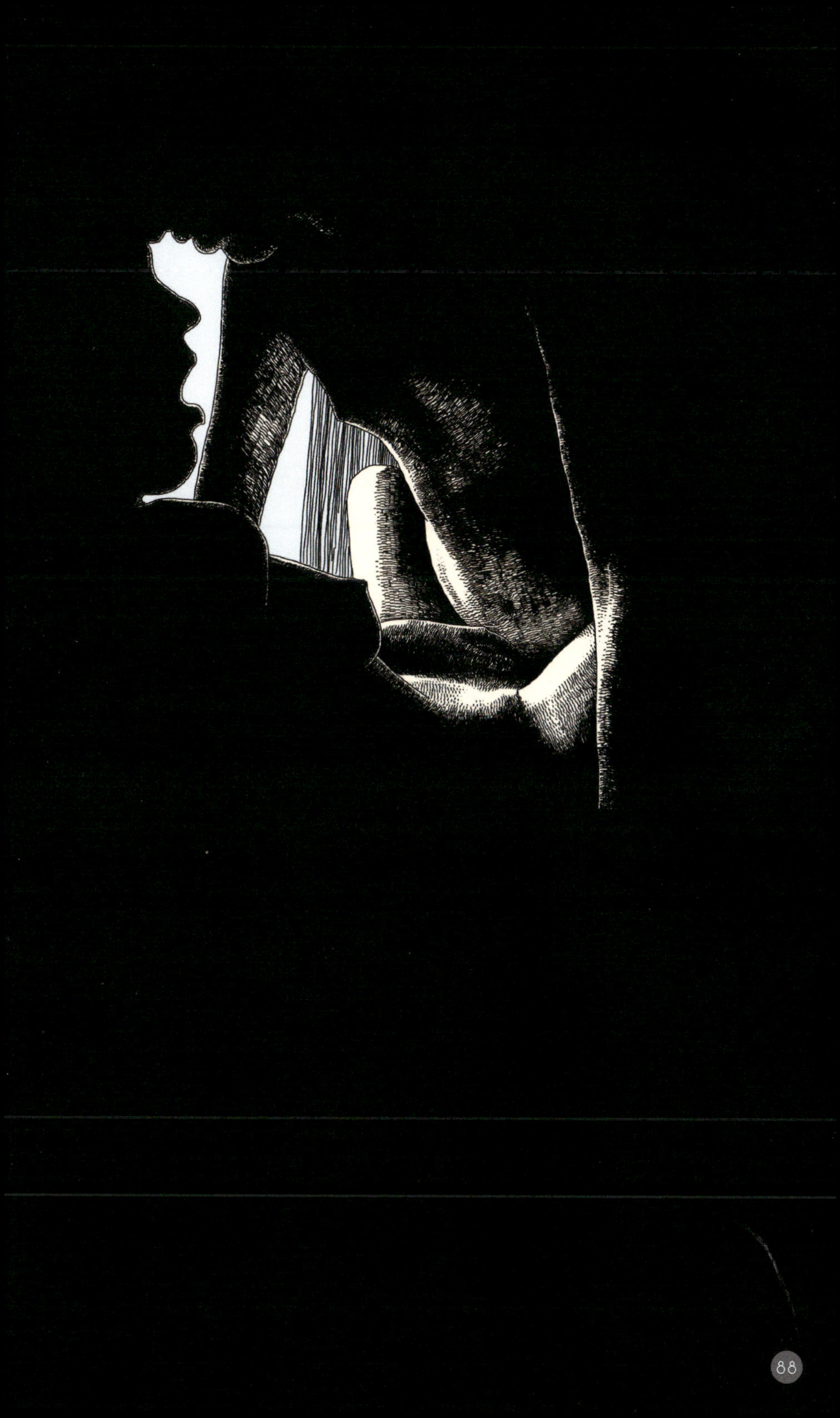